The White Guinea-Pig

Geraldine hadn't wanted the white guinea-pig at all. But then a single, sudden act of sympathy exploded into something difficult and dangerous, like a kiss given to the wrong person.

In fact, Geraldine's whole life is starting to feel oddly out of control. Without warning her parents sell the house, sinister strangers appear, her older sister is torn between two decidedly unusual boyfriends, and Geraldine's neighbour and sort-of-friend Ezra is guarding a terrible secret . . .

The White Guinea-Pig won the 1994 NSW State Literary Award and the 1994 Victorian Premier's Literary Award (Children's Books). It was also short-listed for the 1995 Australian Children's Book of the Year Award (Older Readers).

'A sad tale? Actually not. You'll be moved by the sudden, warm ending; with its lightness and wit, this is a comedy of some depth.'

the *Observer*

URSULA DUBOSARSKY

The White Guinea-Pig

Puffin Books

Puffin Books
Penguin Books Australia Ltd
487 Maroondah Highway PO Box 257
Ringwood, Victoria 3134, Australia
Penguin Books Ltd
Harmondsworth, Middlesex, England
Penguin Putnam Inc.
375 Hudson Street, New York, New York 10014, USA
Penguin Books Canada Limited
10 Alcorn Avenue, Toronto, Ontario, Canada M4V 3B2
Penguin Books (NZ) Ltd
Cnr Rosedale and Airborne Roads, Albany, Auckland, New Zealand
Penguin Books (South Africa) (Pty) Ltd
5 Watkins Street, Denver Ext 4, 2094, South Africa
Penguin Books India (P) Ltd
11, Community Centre, Panchsheel Park, New Delhi 110 017, India

First published by
Penguin Books Australia, 1994
Published in Puffin, 1997
3 5 7 9 10 8 6 4
Copyright © Ursula Dubosarsky, 1994

Typeset in 12/14 Goudy Old Style by Midland Typesetters, Victoria
Made and printed in Australia by Australian Print Group, Maryborough, Victoria

National Library of Australia
Cataloguing-in-Publication data:

Dubosarsky, Ursula, 1961–
The white guinea-pig.

ISBN 014 0366326

1. Guinea-pigs – Juvenile fiction. I. Title.

A823.3

www.puffin.com.au

To dearest Dover Zelig

Dear Father, hear and bless
Thy beasts and singing birds
And guard with tenderness
Small things that have no words.

Anonymous prayer

Contents

Alberta

It was so unfair, the whole business with the white guinea-pig. Geraldine hadn't wanted another guinea-pig at all. In fact, she was busy plotting how she might get rid of the ones she had – swap them, perhaps, for a few uninvolving rubber plants; sell them at the local market; even let them go in a deserted park to fend for themselves.

But then a single, sudden unguarded act of sympathy exploded into something difficult and dangerous she'd never intended, like a kiss given to the wrong person.

It started with a girl at school, Alma – tall and wide with thick white plaits and not even a particular friend of hers – seizing upon her at a vulnerable moment.

'You've got guinea-pigs, haven't you?' said Alma one morning, standing outside the lockers where Geraldine was trying to wedge her oversized maths textbook through the small grey metal door.

'Mmm.' Geraldine nodded. She should have lied. But she did have two guinea-pigs, Milly and Martha, and saw no reason to pretend otherwise.

'Well, have you got room for another?' continued Alma, getting straight to the point. 'Because we're going away for six weeks and I've got to find someone to look after mine.'

'Oh,' said Geraldine, straightening up.

'Dad said if I didn't find anywhere he'd put it in a paper bag and drop a brick on it,' mentioned Alma, adroitly.

Could there be anyone alive, wondered Geraldine, who could say no after hearing a thing like that?

'Oh,' she said.

That was enough for Alma. 'Great,' she said, producing a pink shoe box from her satchel. 'I knew you would.'

She lifted the lid of the box as if to reveal a precious emerald necklace. Geraldine frowned weakly. What had happened in the past fifteen seconds? Had she really landed herself with another guinea-pig? She peered inside the box. It was rather larger than her own two, with long, white hair, like an Abyssinian cat. It twitched its nose and stared at her through pink eyes. Its claws, unseen beneath the wads of fur, made a scratching noise as they shuffled about the cardboard floor of the box.

'It's fat, isn't it?' said Geraldine, uncertainly, strangely nervous of this odd white creature. There must be some way to back out. 'It's not pregnant, is it? Is it a boy or a girl?'

'Female,' admitted Alma. 'But she can't be pregnant. I've had her since she was a baby, all by herself.'

'Maybe she won't get on with mine, then,' said Geraldine, genuinely worried, suddenly imagining ear-piercing shrieks and spurts of blood emerging from the cage in their normally peaceful backyard.

But Alma waved this aside. 'She's as gentle as a lamb,' she said. 'She sleeps in my bed.'

Well, she's not sleeping in mine, thought Geraldine. 'What's her name?' she asked, knowing she had submitted and would never find the strength to retreat.

'Alberta,' replied Alma. 'All the women in my family have names beginning with "A".'

The bell rang for the next lesson. Alma tossed back her ribboned plaits. 'Just for six weeks,' she called back at Geraldine as she disappeared down the corridor. 'She won't be any trouble.'

Geraldine had no time to answer, no time even to open her mouth. She crouched down next to her locker, shoe box in hand. This must be how people felt when orphaned babies were left in baskets on their doorsteps, this uncomfortable mixture of pity and resentment. She still had the remains of a peanut-butter sandwich she'd been eating for morning tea in her hand, so she gingerly lifted the lid and offered it to her new charge. Alberta snatched the bread greedily with her front claws and gulped it down.

Six weeks, Geraldine thought, trying to console herself. But six weeks, she was to discover, could change everything.

The Pigs

Geraldine's father always referred to Milly and Martha as 'the pigs'. This sometimes alarmed visitors, when he would say, 'Have you seen our pigs out the back?' or, 'The lawn's never been the same since Gerry brought those pigs home.'

'The pigs' were two small chubby guinea-pigs that looked like a pair of ill-matched, mobile mittens with claws. They were brown and white and black, and, as pets go, rather disappointing.

Geraldine had a lot of experience with pets. Sometimes it felt as if most of her conscious life had been spent in search of the perfect pet. It started at the age of three, when she'd found half a dead lizard on top of a brick in the back garden – its tail must have been eaten off by a bird.

It was very small, scarcely the width of one of her own tiny fingers, and already a trail of ants was making a calm and ruthless track towards the carcass.

Geraldine remembered very clearly the wave of compassion that she'd felt (a new emotion in that young life), as she'd picked it up gently and put it in an empty matchbox with a piece of cotton wool as a pillow. She didn't realise it was dead, not being at all clear what dead meant anyway, but thought that it just needed a little rest. So she put it in the fridge, in the side box next to the butter.

Then she forgot about it, of course, becoming quickly preoccupied by the television and lunch and colouring books, until about a week later when her mother found it there and was memorably distressed. Rather as her father had been when Geraldine hid a raw egg under the sofa cushions, hoping it would hatch into a baby chick. She'd forgotten to mention it to anyone, though, so when he plonked himself down to watch television that night, it had made a challenging sort of mess.

The years passed, and Geraldine lost interest in reptiles and eggs, and discovered dogs. She began to feel a compulsion to go up to every dog she saw and pat the top of its head and scratch it under its ears, looking into its wet eyes as if to reassure it that she at least loved it and was its eternal friend. Naturally enough, lonely, or perhaps not so

6

lonely but hungry, dogs started to follow her ho.
which delighted Geraldine but no one else in h
family. They would ring up the owner or the
council and watch in cold-blooded satisfaction as
the poor betrayed creature was dragged off howling. Well, sometimes howling; at other times they
seemed quite relieved to go.

Geraldine's family were not animal lovers.
Despite constant campaigning, she had not yet
managed to convince them to let her have a dog
of her own. Have a cat, they suggested, perhaps
thinking of all those television commercials where
the family cat appears silently at meal times, bends
its head obediently over a plastic bowl, and then
runs off by itself to do more interesting things. But
this was precisely why Geraldine did not want a
cat. She wanted to feel appreciated. Adored.
Worshipped. Dogs did that. Any dog.

On her ninth birthday, as a kind of compromise,
they gave her a bird in a cage, a bright blue budgie
called Paul. But Geraldine was frightened by the
feelings Paul aroused in her. Chiefly, he irritated
her. She wanted him to be happy, but he was not
happy. She wanted to love him, but she didn't. And
he definitely didn't love her. Every time she came
near him, whistling and murmuring, his heart
began visibly pumping with stress and he shuffled
to the furthest end of his perch, as if awaiting an
executioner. What terrible things could she be
whistling in bird language? she wondered, and so

7

she stopped whistling after a while and stuck to English.

She decided that he must want to be free, out of the bounds of his nice clean cage, so she tried letting him out to fly around her bedroom. Well, it was not so much a case of letting him out as thrusting him out, and then watching him attach his trembling claws to the curtain rod and refuse to move.

Then she tried hanging his cage in a tree in the front garden, so at least he could pretend he was free. But he only seemed to grow more and more attached to the little yellow mirror with the bell hanging off it that he spent so much time pathetically trilling at. As a last desperate act of beneficence, she started deliberately leaving his cage door open, so that he might take it into his own head to fly away into liberty. Day after day he ignored it. It drove Geraldine mad.

Until one afternoon, when she came home from school and found to her great relief that he was gone. The cage hanging from the branch was empty. Her mother tried to comfort her (how little she knew!), saying that perhaps someone had stolen him. Geraldine was inclined to agree – it hardly seemed feasible, given his general disposition, that Paul had spent the last eight months eyeing the open door and then finally taken a plunge into nature.

No, someone passing by had spied him hanging

there and taken him home to live in their nice airy aviary with lots of other birds, and he would at last be happy. Or so she kept reminding herself every time she was visited by visions of his poor blue feathery body quaking in the jaws of a local cat.

After Paul, she kept fish. She saved up her pocket-money and bought a black one and a gold one from a department-store pet shop, as well as the tank, some plants and three sea-snails who died on the bus on the way home. Well, if Paul had been over-responsive to her advances, this was not the problem with the fish. Did they even know she was alive? Did they wonder where their daily supply of fish-flakes came from? Did they care about anyone else at all? All they did was swim about all day long, opening their mouths in a perfect 'O'. She used to stare at them, fascinated how anything could be satisfied with a life so relentlessly tranquil.

Her next-door neighbour, Ezra, however, informed her that she was quite mistaken. Fish lead very stimulating lives, he claimed. They have no memory, so every time they see each other, they are as surprised as if it is the very first time. On learning this, Geraldine quickly revised her judgement. They saw each other a hundred times a day at least, she calculated, swimming round and around, so they must in fact live in a state of almost constant excitement. No wonder they were always saying 'O'.

In the end, like all living things, fortunately for

Geraldine, they died. She was as unmoved by their deaths as by Paul's disappearance, apart from the relief she felt knowing she would not have to spend every Saturday morning changing their stagnant and strong-smelling water. She was frightened by their floating bodies, though, and quickly scooped them up in a coffee-strainer and tossed them out the window into a bed of white azaleas. The tiny thud on the earth below made her shiver. 'Although you're perfectly happy to eat fish and chips,' Ezra pointed out, in his usual annoying way. 'Or don't you think of that as a dead body?'

Ezra was eleven, six months younger than Geraldine, and had been her next-door neighbour for three years. It was only in the last year or so that he had become interested in Animal Liberation. Now he was always getting newsletters and reading thin-paged recycled grey booklets on the bus. He was against having pets – he said it was undignified for both parties concerned. He'd been against the fish, and he was strongly opposed to her guinea-pigs, which had become Geraldine's next venture, also brought home from the pet shop.

'What's wrong with having guinea-pigs?' argued Geraldine, just for the sake of conversation, not with any hope of convincing Ezra otherwise. 'I'll look after them. I won't neglect them or anything.'

'But you won't respect them as sentient beings,' said Ezra.

Ezra was always going on about sentient beings –
it was one of his things. When he'd first used the
expression, Geraldine asked her sixteen-year-old
sister, Violetta, what it meant, and Violetta had
said it was something that had feelings.

'What sort of feelings?' asked Geraldine.

'Oh, all sorts, I suppose,' said Violetta. 'Pleasure,
pain, love, that sort of thing,' and she sighed, being
a rather sentient being herself.

Ezra was a vegetarian, like the other people in
Animal Liberation. He was a particular kind of
vegetarian, though, the kind who only ate non-
sentient beings, so it was important to know what
was and what wasn't. Ezra said that oysters were
not sentient beings, so it was all right to eat them,
but snails were, so they were forbidden. Not that
Geraldine had ever been tempted to eat either.
And how could you tell, she wondered, that a snail
felt love and an oyster didn't? But Ezra would get
that impatient look on his face. 'You don't understand the principle,' he'd say. 'And you say you care
about animals. You don't really care about them
at all. You just use them for your own pleasure,
if you think they look nice.'

Geraldine was ashamed then, because she knew
it was true. Why had she gone and bought the
guinea-pigs in the first place? Certainly not because
she respected them as sentient beings, but because
they were fluffy and fat and had sweet little
wrinkling noses and looked as though they should

have a key on their tummies that would play 'Waltzing Matilda' when you turned it round. Perhaps that's what she should have spent her money on – a clockwork koala. Because now that she had got used to poor Milly and Martha, it was true, like all the other pets she had acquired in a fit of sentiment, she was sick of them.

She looked after them well, she could at least console herself with that. Even Ezra had to agree. Although he disapproved, he took a dedicated interest in their well-being and made periodic inspections of their cage and food supply. Geraldine used to feel like a mother being assessed by a baby health nurse on these occasions, and true to form Ezra usually managed to find some grudging compliment to make about the shine of their fur or the sharpness of their teeth.

'How long do guinea-pigs live?' she asked him one day, in feigned indifference.

'Three years,' he replied without hesitation. Ezra knew the life span of everything, even germs. 'Of course, animals in captivity live a lot longer than in their natural state.'

'Oh,' said Geraldine. How very depressing. Milly and Martha looked as if they were positively thriving on their captivity. They never appeared sluggish or dull-eyed, or showed any other encouraging signs of approaching death she'd read about in various pet manuals at the library. How much longer would she be burdened with them? Because they were a burden to her. She tried to feel other, more St Francis-like emotions, but failed.

The truth was, of course, Milly and Martha didn't care about her any more than the fish had. They wouldn't care if she lived or died. They didn't even recognise her as she dutifully plodded out the back every day with a wad of lettuce and a handful of guinea-pig pellets. When they saw her, they huddled together under the blanket in the corner of the cage she'd constructed out of an old kitchen cupboard and some chicken-wire, only creeping out to gobble down the food after she'd gone back inside.

Not only were Milly and Martha emotionally unsatisfactory, they caused a certain amount of family friction as well. This was because of the lawn. Before Milly and Martha arrived, there had been a pleasant sloping green expanse to look out at from the kitchen window. Now there was only a patchwork of dry yellow oblongs where they had eaten through the chicken-wire at the bottom of their cage. Geraldine, when she made the cage, had imagined them taking an occasional nibble of the fresh stalks as a supplement to their diet of salad and pellets, but she had been sadly ignorant of the eating habits of guinea-pigs. It soon became apparent that Milly and Martha had absolutely no control over their appetites. They ate and they ate and they ate. She moved the cage every day to a new patch of grass, like rotating crops, and every day they ate it down to the dirt. What they saw, they ate. It could have been their family motto.

And it was the lawn that really worried Geraldine as she carefully carried the shoe box home that afternoon on the ferry and then the bus. Not whether Alberta was pregnant or incompatible with Milly and Martha, but the fact that she hadn't rung and asked her parents if she could have another one, even for six weeks. She hadn't, because she knew they would say no.

They would say no because of the lawn. And the lawn mattered a lot now, because they were going to sell their house. And they were going to sell their house because Geraldine's father had gone bankrupt.

3

The Smuggling

Geraldine's father was a businessman – he sold toys. At one stage in their family's life, he'd made a lot of money from doing this. He had a gift for toys, an eye. His own parents had started the business before World War II, which seemed to Geraldine a very long time ago. When her father grew up, and his parents died, he took over.

Their house was always full of toys, samples brought back from factories all over the world. Wooden toys, metal toys, soft toys, toy cars, musical boxes, strange little mechanical toys that you wound up or pressed buttons or pushed levers to get them to flash or jump or spin. Whenever her father brought home a new toy to show them, her first question always was, 'What does it do?'

Because the kinds of toys her father liked always 'did' something, had some unguessable function to perform.

Geraldine's father was a roundish sort of man with romantically long brown hair. His name was Wolfgang. 'Wolf' for short, but there was nothing at all crafty or voracious about him. In the evenings in summer he would fetch his guitar from the laundry cupboard and sit on the back porch, singing 'Georgy Girl' and 'Yellow Submarine' to what was left of his lawn, as he believed singing was good for plants. Geraldine liked to hear him sing, but he had stopped since he became bankrupt.

Geraldine had no idea why her father's toys were no longer making a lot of money, but were instead losing money in a drastic way. Had the world changed so much from what it was before World War II? Apparently yes. Children now wanted things with silicon chips, or toys that gave you an education. Well, their parents did, anyway. Geraldine's father had never been very strong in those lines. They didn't seem to suit him.

Her parents had not told her that their toy business was no longer making any money – she had found this out from Violetta. Violetta always knew things. Geraldine had never been sure whether this was because their parents actually told her more because she was older, or just because Violetta was a more expert eavesdropper. Anyway, she'd come home from school one day and gone into Violetta's room to tell her about an excursion her class was going on to the Warrumbungles, and Violetta had said, 'You can't ask for money for it, you know. Not with things as they are.'

'What things?' Geraldine had asked, puzzled.

'Dad's going broke.' Violetta dropped her voice to a whisper. 'We're going to have to sell everything.'

'Going broke,' repeated Geraldine.

'They're even going to sell the house, you know,' divulged Violetta. 'And all the furniture. To pay the creditors.'

Geraldine was horrified. Where were they going to live, then? And what would they sleep on, or eat their breakfast from? Would they have to keep their milk in a bucket of water outside, like people did in the olden days, before fridges? Would her father stand on the outside ledge of a tall building in town and threaten to jump off, like she'd seen in old movies about the Wall Street Crash?

After that conversation with Violetta, Geraldine had expected to come home any day and find a removalist truck outside with all their furniture in it, and a man counting up the money with little dollar-signs where his eyes should be. But she discovered that bankruptcy was not like that – it didn't happen that quickly. It was slow and destructive, like a chronic illness.

Geraldine had always loved living in a house surrounded by toys, but now they took on a sinister aspect. The levers and shiny buttons and happy clown faces each seemed to play their little part in her father's mysterious downfall. Her mother grew thin and her father grew fat; her father slept badly and her mother, who had never slept well, even worse. They closed the glass doors of the dining-room in the evenings and talked softly together. They said nothing about it at all to Geraldine. They wouldn't, of course, they wouldn't want to worry her. Life is sad enough, her mother told her once, without worrying about things you can do nothing about.

How could she bring another guinea-pig into such a home? Just imagine the lawn – with two it was bad enough, but a third, equally, possibly more, ravenous? Her mother had asked her only that weekend whether there was some way the pigs could be encouraged to eat less. 'We have to sell the house, you know, darling, so everything's got to look its best.' Well, I didn't know, actually, Geraldine felt like saying. How am I supposed to know if you don't tell me? But she said nothing.

When she got home that afternoon with Alberta in the shoe box under her arm, she found her mother in the dining-room, staring down at long sheets of paper spread across the table, with numbers typed on them. Carefully camouflaging the shoe box behind her school bag, Geraldine went over and kissed her.

'Dad asleep?' she asked, hopefully.

Her mother grunted. 'He had a bad night,' she said. 'Best not to disturb him.'

Well, that's two of them out of the way, thought Geraldine with satisfaction. And Violetta was not likely to be a problem – she was sure to be busy studying. Violetta was always studying – she was terribly brainy and in her last year of school. Geraldine crept down the corridor and peeped into her sister's room. There she was, frowning in her glasses.

She heard Geraldine, but didn't turn around. 'Physics test,' she muttered in explanation.

So the family was well buried – Violetta in physics, her father in blankets and her mother in sheets of long white paper. Geraldine slipped out to the laundry and creaked open the back door. Alberta, obviously restless, scuffled her feet on the bottom of the box.

On one side of the devastated brown and yellow field of grass sloping down to the fence of Ezra's place was a lemon tree with an old tyre strung up in one of its branches for a swing. It was a tree generous with its fruit – perhaps rather too generous, as lemon trees often are. Violetta had read in a cookery column that lemon juice brings out the natural flavour of food, so they'd had quite a lot of unusual meals – or, rather, usual meals with an unexpected citrus aftertaste. Not to mention all the jars of lemon-butter, bowls of lemon-delicious pudding and jugs and jugs of home-made lemonade, like you get in Lebanese restaurants, that Violetta also went in for.

Anyway, Geraldine had dragged the cage under the lemon tree that morning, thinking that there was so little grass growing beneath its heavy branches that the pigs could scarcely do any more harm. As she walked over to it, shoe box in arm, smelling an odour of lemon mixed with guinea-pig droppings, Milly and Martha dived under the blue tartan blanket in their normal fashion, quivering in anticipation.

'They must think I've got something to eat,' said Geraldine to herself. This was not particularly insightful of her, as that was all they ever did think. Fear and greed were the only not-very-endearing emotions she inspired in them. She hoped it would not be too much of a shock, this sudden white visitor, to their uneventful lives. She lifted up the cupboard door, which acted as the lid of the cage, and peered in.

'What are you doing?'

Geraldine swung around. It was Ezra, leaning over the back fence, looking disapproving, like in a movie she'd seen of John Knox gazing balefully over a stone wall at Mary Queen of Scots.

'Oh,' she said.

'You've got another one, haven't you?' he asked outright. Ezra never dropped hints, or allowed opportunity for escape.

'I didn't want it!' said Geraldine. 'This girl at school forced it on me!'

'You can't possibly keep three in there. There's not enough space,' replied Ezra, adding mercilessly, 'Do you know what happens to rodents when they're overcrowded?'

Geraldine did not know, but she knew she did not want to know. Ezra was the sort of person who always managed to include all the nasty details that are impossible to forget; that keep floating back into your mind like hunger.

'It's only for six weeks,' she said, crossly. 'While this girl's on holidays.'

Ezra stared at her. 'It'll end in cannibalism,' he said. 'I won't tell you how it'll begin.'

'Look,' retorted Geraldine, 'her father was going to kill it if she didn't find somewhere.' She took the lid off the shoe box and went over to the fence to show him. It was dusk, but Alberta's fur shone even brighter than in daylight. Ezra looked darkly into the two pink eyes. He didn't ask its name. He didn't believe in giving animals names. He frowned and hesitated, then looked up at Geraldine. 'If you ask me,' he pronounced, 'there's something odd about it.'

Geraldine snatched the box back. 'What do you mean?'

Ezra shrugged. 'I'm not sure. It looks strange to me, that's all.'

'Oh, come off it!' Geraldine snapped. Now that

Ezra had criticised Alberta, Geraldine found herself wanting to defend her new foster-child, to protect her from an unappreciative and uncaring world. She reached in with her hand and drew out the white mass of blood, fur and bone, and held her up in the disappearing sunlight.

'Poor little thing,' she muttered, uncertainly, as when you had a good look at her, there was nothing in the least vulnerable about Alberta. Her pink eyes were alarmingly acute, her claws over-sharp, and her long white hair unnaturally bright, almost fluorescent. Quickly, Geraldine placed her gently on the chicken-wire on the bottom of the cage, next to the trembling, squeaking blanket of Milly and Martha.

She straightened up, and looked over at Ezra, feeling belligerent. He raised his eyebrows, infuriatingly.

'There,' said Geraldine, turning and addressing Alberta. 'Makes a nice change from a shoe box, doesn't it?'

Milly and Martha showed no signs of emerging from the refuge of their blanket. Alberta ignored Geraldine, sniffed a little, moved forward, found a half-chewed piece of carrot end and started to nibble on it with a certain disdain.

Geraldine pulled her blazer more tightly around her shoulders as the night winds rose.

'Well, good night,' she said casually to Ezra, determined not to pursue the subject of Alberta any further with him.

'Good night,' Ezra replied, always polite. He did have good manners, despite everything. Everyone always said so.

Geraldine walked quickly back to the house, not looking around. She wanted to watch television, or listen to a tape. Soon it would be time for 'I Love Lucy'.

It occurred to her with irritation as she wedged her way in through the baskets of unironed clothes in the laundry, that she'd forgotten to ask Ezra not to mention anything about Alberta to her family, or his, for that matter. She was pretty sure she could keep it a secret as long as he didn't say anything. Her parents wouldn't notice what colour the guinea-pigs were, and they were usually under the blankets anyway. And Violetta wouldn't have a clue – she never even looked out the window. Just as long as Ezra kept his mouth shut.

She'd tell him tomorrow – she'd had more than enough of his disapproval for one day. He would have gone inside now, anyway. She'd tell him at the bus-stop in the morning.

And she flopped herself down on the sofa in the living-room in front of the television, never realising that she'd left the lid of the guinea-pig cage wide open to the sky, like a trapdoor from an underground cell.

4

Tory

Ezra stood in the darkening yard for a moment after Geraldine had gone indoors, watching the guinea-pigs graze, bobbing their heads up and down and squealing softly in pleasure. He noticed the open door of the cage. Typical. She was always leaving it open. He chewed on his thumbnail thoughtfully for a moment. Then he put his hands in his pockets and turned to go inside his own house.

In the living-room, his parents were, as usual, watching *Paint Your Wagon* on the video. At least, his father was watching while his mother kept him company.

To look at, Ezra's parents were like larger versions of Ezra. They were both brown-haired, medium-sized and they both wore glasses. They also both worked in travel agencies, so the house was decorated with wooden-backed posters of solid, dependable locations, like London, Washington, and Rome, which their respective offices had discarded in favour of Jamaica, Mozambique and Vanuatu.

Ezra's father sat in an armchair, his mother on the sofa, calmly making shapes with a macramé needle and cream-coloured thread. Ezra slouched down next to her, resting his head on her shoulder, thinking about Geraldine. That girl was impossible. Another cavie! (Ezra preferred to call them 'cavies', as they did in natural history books.) And such an odd-looking one too – so large – what if it was in the later stages of pregnancy? That'd give her a shock all right. Another half-a-dozen little hairless rodents to deal with.

The deep, deep voice on the film was now singing the song 'I Was Born Under a Wand'ring Star'. Ezra wondered idly, as he often did, what it really would have been like to live on a wild Californian goldfield – not with any personal yearning, just curiosity. His father watched this same film sometimes several times a week, and now after seeing it so often, the characters had almost become real to Ezra, like Bible stories.

The noise of a plane passing overhead momentarily blocked out the music. Ezra's mother raised her eyes to the ceiling, perhaps well-wishing one of her many clients who could be on board, floating high above the city, looking down on the huge stretch of tiny lights flashing like an earthbound galaxy. Ezra disliked planes; their noise, their shape, their colour and the rows of square windows. A plane overhead for him was like a black cat crossing his path. It made him shiver.

He stood up and went over to the window, drawing the curtains slightly, looking out over Geraldine's garden. He felt unsettled, his brain racing in no particular direction. Perhaps if he did some cooking – some ginger-crunch biscuits, or some melting moments. Ezra had quite a sweet tooth and found a certain solace in cooking: following the printed directions, measuring substances of different consistencies into bowls of various sizes, heating things to prescribed temperatures, mixing, spooning, baking and finally, of course, eating.

Ezra let the curtain drop and wandered down to his room. They would be having dinner soon, so it was hardly the time to start making biscuits. He sat down at his desk with the shelf of books above it and picked up an Animal Liberation pamphlet about pain-free cosmetics that he'd received in the mail that afternoon. But he couldn't concentrate. For reasons he was unsure of, but which seemed somehow connected with that strange white guinea-pig next door, he was thinking too much about Tory.

Tory was his baby sister. Really his baby sister. Some people say baby sister just to mean younger sister, even when the sister is quite grown-up, with children of her own. But Tory was a real baby sister. She had always been a baby and always would be. She never grew up, because she was run over by a utility truck when she was only two-and-a-half years old.

That was three years ago, before they moved to this house. Three terrible years. It often puzzled Ezra – you would think the first day, month, year would be the worst, easing off gradually, like the effect of alcohol, but it didn't seem to work that way. For him, at any rate, the first day was the least terrible. The day Tory was killed. Afterwards was far worse.

Tory was brown-haired and small, like the rest of them. If she had grown up, she would have needed glasses, like the rest of them. Tory was very sweet and pink and soft and Ezra loved her terribly. He was more than six years older than her, so he could carry her, and put her to bed, and read to her. He dressed her up in funny clothes, painted her face with crayons, tickled her, shouted at her, told her to stop crying at once or he would smack her. He turned the hose on her, gave her sweet things to eat, scolded her, hid her socks, kissed her, hated her, was jealous of her, adored her. Ezra did not have many friends, but here he found he had a home-grown friend, who would never leave him,

27

who would always be glad to see him and want to have him around.

The morning Tory left him for good it was raining. Tory liked the rain. She always wanted to go out and play in it; find the muddiest spot in the garden, and make nice brown foot- and hand-prints right through the house. Ezra remembered waking up to the dark grey light and hearing the gutters dripping like a chorus of metronomes. He rolled over and whispered, 'Tory! It's raining!'

Tory slept in the same room as Ezra, in a red wooden cot. She loved her cot and so did Ezra – he could pretend she was a dangerous wild animal at the zoo that was always trying to escape and tear people to shreds.

'Tory!'

Tory was a late sleeper. Often Ezra would lie in bed in the early mornings watching her through the red bars, stretched out across her mattress, pillow and blankets tossed aside impatiently at some stage during the night. She made such faces as she slept: frowning, twisting her mouth, pushing her hands across her face. He loved just to lie still and watch her.

'Tory! Wake up! It's raining!'

It was a Sunday morning. Ezra could hear his father making coffee in the kitchen. His mother would be in bed reading or writing letters to her sisters. Tory wrinkled her nose in distaste at the intrusion of her brother's voice, and rolled over, banging her forehead on the edge of the cot. At once she opened her mouth in complaint.

Ezra jumped out of bed and went over, taking her up in his arms. Her nappy was wet through, of course, so he began to pull off the sticky plastic tabs to let her run unburdened through the house. She wriggled crankily, but let him do it. She licked the tears from her cheeks and smiled.

How, Ezra wondered, could he be so sure of every detail of what happened that morning, when it must have been exactly the same as so many others? How could he know he was remembering the right one, and not mixing it up? But he could scarcely bring to mind all those other precious days, and he was left with the hard small stone of that final Sunday.

'Pitter patter rain is falling down!' Tory sang, a monotonous song she had learned at childcare, but which seemed to her endlessly entertaining. 'Pitter patter rain is falling down!'

Ezra made her breakfast – Weetbix with warm milk and brown sugar. She liked it all mushed up, one caramel-coloured blur of food. She fed herself with her own pink plastic spoon.

'Is it good?' said Ezra's father, squeezing her shoulders. 'Is it delicious?'

'Tory!' called their mother from the bedroom. 'Come in and give me a kiss!'

Ezra made himself raisin toast, and ate three pieces. The rain was easing. He decided to go for a bike ride. Sunday mornings were always good for riding, as there was so little traffic, and he loved the way the wheels on the wet roads made the water shoot up with a splashing whirr on his legs. Tory would be cross – she didn't like him to go out without her, but perhaps they'd let her watch television that morning, to keep her out of the mud and give them a bit of peace.

He put his plate on the sink, then went back to his room to get a jumper. Tory was in his parents' bedroom, screeching and laughing. He didn't say goodbye, just muttered to his father, who was tossing coffee grounds into the front flower-bed, that he was going out on his bike. The handlebars were cold and wet, and he pushed the front gate shut behind him with his foot and started down the black shining hill.

He rode around the almost-silent suburban streets, turning circles and figures of eight on the wide roads, feeling the wet leaves of low hanging branches brush into his face, leaving drops on his cheeks like cold tears. An elderly man with a sack was delivering leaflets; some childen he knew by sight were playing hopscotch and throwing stones on the footpath. The shops were closed, but there was a pile of papers and an honesty box outside the newsagent. In the distance, but not too far off, he heard a siren – police, ambulance, fire? He was never sure which was which. The minister, in black shirt and trousers, was carrying a cardboard box into the back of the sandstone church, talking and nodding to his wife who ran along beside him. Ezra span his wheels with pleasure by all of them, and began to feel warm and thirsty.

He must have been out nearly half an hour. By the time he came home, it was all over. Tory was dead. He didn't turn the corner and see it happen, he wasn't even able to call out, 'Tory! Be careful!' He didn't know what happened, and he was never able to ask.

He turned past the church, braking down the black tar hill to their house. He saw the ambulance and a police car. He heard wailing, human wailing, not a siren. He had never heard anyone wail before, and this was his mother, though he didn't recognise her voice.

He jumped off his bike. Tory was on a stretcher in the ambulance, and his parents beside her, kissing her. She was covered with blood. She was broken and grotesque. She was undeniably dead. He turned his face. He never saw her again. He didn't kiss her. He hadn't even bothered to kiss her goodbye when he left the house that morning.

The rest of the day, he scarcely knew what happened. He stayed near his parents, he knew that, because he remembered how tightly his father held his hand all day, so much that at night his fingers were bruised and throbbing.

He thought he remembered seeing the white truck that ran her over parked outside their house,

and the man who drove it, and the police talking
to him, but he couldn't be sure. Perhaps his
memory had just made it up afterwards. He didn't
ask his parents – not that day, not ever – what had
happened, how Tory came to be on the road, how
the driver hadn't seen her, were they inside, were
they in the garden? Did Tory scream, did she cry
out? He knew some things, just from listening, but
he was told nothing.

Tory was dead. It had even been reported in the
newspaper: four small smudgy black and white
lines. Your name in the paper. People cut those
sort of things out and stick them in scrap-books
to show their friends. Had his parents cut it out?
Had they just thrown the paper away, wrapped
potato peel in it? What could you do with it? Ezra
remembered the time when he had nerved himself
into throwing out a copy of the Bible. The pages
were tattered and half-unreadable, still he expected God to strike him dead any moment. But
it was Tory who was struck dead, and ruined all
their lives.

Ezra didn't go to her funeral, he didn't want to.
He went to school instead, and sent his parents
alone. Tory was buried that Thursday afternoon.

They moved house after it happened. Their new
suburb was just the same and even the house itself
was not all that different, but at least it was a house
that had never known Tory. And they lived next
door to and went to school with and bought milk

and bread from people who had never known Tory. She was their own deep, private secret.

It was because of Tory that Ezra became interested in Animal Liberation. He'd found a pamphlet in the local library, and for him the message was very simple and true – life is valuable and nothing should die unnecessarily. Oh how true it was. How he believed it.

He told his parents he was no longer going to eat meat or wear leather shoes. He sent in his Animal Liberation membership, torn off from the bottom of the library pamphlet, and started getting letters and phone calls from adults after nine o'clock at night. His mother brought home a paperback recipe book, *Delicious and Nutritious Ways to Feed a Growing Vegetarian*, that the doctor had apparently recommended and which Ezra thought made him sound like some kind of exotic South American lizard. Then he began going to Animal Liberation meetings, which his father dutifully drove him to, as if he were taking him to the Wolf Cubs or miniature-car racing.

Ezra was always the youngest by far at these meetings, and he never said anything, beyond a 'hello' and 'thank you' for biscuits made without animal products and cups of honey-sweet tea. They all smiled at him and called him by name and some of them even shook his hand when he arrived.

Ezra couldn't have said he positively enjoyed the meetings, but he got used to them. There was always a lot of quarrelling in rather formal language, over what letter to write or whose conference to picket, and then someone would read out something outrageous or wonderful from a book or magazine, and they would discuss it. Well, fight about it, particularly two elderly ladies who always came together and apparently even lived together, but who seemed to have distinctly different but equally firmly held opinions on just about everything. Sometimes the rest of the members would just leave them to it, and sit back in the bean-bags and armchairs, munching on the sweet food, until eventually someone would look at their watch and start clearing their throat and suggest a vote of thanks to their host for this month's invaluable meeting.

Ezra sighed. He had a photo of Tory on his bookshelf, and he looked at it often, without tears. His parents had photos too, throughout the house, some of them framed, some of them with him in them as well, his arms around her little shoulders, or trying to carry her along the beach. He laid his head gently on his pillow, and looked up at the ceiling, letting the pamphlet about pain-free cosmetics fall onto the carpeted floor. He placed his hand over his chest and began to count his ribs.

'Ezra! Telephone! It's Simon!' His mother called him from the kitchen. Clicking his tongue, as though he had been interrupted from an important business conference, he got himself up and went out. Simon was a man – well, a boy, really; he had just started university – from Animal Liberation. He was doing a degree in medieval Nordic languages, he told Ezra when they first met, and was very impressed by the advances made in animal welfare in Sweden. He'd taken a liking to Ezra, perhaps on account of his youth rather than his charms, as Ezra was generally taciturn and non-committal in conversation. Simon usually rang Ezra a week or so before each meeting to check that he was coming.

'Hello?' said Ezra cautiously, as he picked up the phone.

'Ezra! Simon here.'

'Hello,' repeated Ezra.

'Right, well. I'm ringing to ask a bit of a favour, actually.'

'Yes.'

'Yes, well. You know Shirley?'

'Yes,' admitted Ezra. Shirley was one of their fellow Liberation members.

'Well, she's got chicken-pox.'

'Oh.' Chicken-pox? Ezra frowned. Surely only children got that. Shirley must be at least fifty. 'Are you sure it's not smallpox?'

'And she can't have this month's meeting at her place, of course,' continued Simon, ignoring this. 'And we thought perhaps you could have it at your place instead.'

'Oh.'

'Usual time, you know, three o'clock. Just for an hour or so.'

'I'd have to ask my parents,' said Ezra, in what he hoped was a discouraging tone. But this was lost on Simon, who only ever seemed to hear the words people said, not the voice they said them in.

'Great! I'd have it here, but my situation's pretty impossible, you know.'

Simon lived at the university, in a tall grey building he shared with about one hundred and fifty other students. Ezra would have thought the university was an ideal place to hold a meeting, with all those box-like rooms, and rows and rows of folding chairs.

'Okay then, Ezra. Thanks. I'll let the others know. See you on Saturday.'

Ezra laid the phone on its rest, twisting his lips. He went out to the living-room.

'A meeting? Here?' said Ezra's father when he told them, holding the pause button over *Paint Your Wagon*.

'How many people, Ezra?' his mother asked, anxious. 'Will they make a lot of noise?' she added, perhaps thinking of televised reports of fierce protests outside fur boutiques.

'I don't know, about ten, I suppose,' Ezra shrugged.

'Animal Liberation,' Ezra's father said, thoughtfully. 'I see.'

'Everyone takes turns, do they, darling?' asked

36

his mother. 'I mean, you have to do your bit.'

'They bring food,' said Ezra. 'We'll just have to make the cups of tea and stuff.'

'Animal Liberation,' Ezra's father repeated, seemingly unable to think of anything else to say, certainly not a yes or no.

'I'm sure it'll be fine,' Ezra's mother decided at last. 'We'll just have to keep out of your way, that's all.'

Ezra's father looked from his son to his wife, eyebrows raised, with a nervous smile. Then he released the pause button, and the gaudy goldfields of California sprang back into sound and motion. The three of them turned their eyes to the screen obediently. But perhaps that night with less certainty of refuge than usual.

··· 5 ···

The Escape

Geraldine woke up late the next morning. She'd
been troubled by unpleasant dreams – well, dreams
are always unpleasant, but these ones lingered
uncomfortably long in her conscious mind and
through her breakfast of toast and honey and milk.

The dreams were about Alberta. An outsized,
angel-white Alberta. An Alberta who found her
way into their living-room to complain about the
glare from the windows that was giving her a
headache, and why didn't they get themselves
some proper blinds? And Geraldine's mother had
apologised: 'I'm so sorry, Roberta, we're too poor
to buy any,' and the white guinea-pig had flashed
her wicked front teeth and replied frostily, 'It's
Alberta, if you don't mind.'

What could this mean? She could ask Violetta,

who'd read books about the meaning of dreams – well, she'd read books about the meaning of everything, really. But Violetta's interpretations always seemed worse than the dreams themselves – it might be better not to know.

Why on earth should she dream about Alberta in the living-room, safely tucked up in her father's favourite armchair, ordering everyone about? Surely, it would be more sensible to dream of Alberta getting eaten by a dog, or dying suddenly of heart failure. Guinea-pigs did get heart failure, after all, she'd read it in one of those pet-care books. She'd even gone so far as imagining how she might bring such a thing on in Milly and Martha – a diet of chips and cream-cakes, perhaps, or a loud unexpected noise . . .

In any case, she was too late getting to the bus-stop to talk to Ezra about keeping his mouth shut on the subject of Alberta. The bus-stop was the only place Ezra would speak with Geraldine in public. That was because there was no one else there, except Violetta, going over her notes on Chaucer or the laws of inertia. Once he got on the bus, he was unapproachable. He sat next to a boy younger than him from a different school, and together they chewed gobs of gum while they read war magazines, blowing out huge unappetising pink bubbles.

The bus took them down to the wharf where the big blue and white ferry was harnessed, waiting to take its load of school children and office workers into the city. The boys Ezra's age from his school lounged about outside smoking cigarettes and talking about things that embarrassed him. He and the bubblegum boy sat inside with all the murmuring adults.

Geraldine sat outside on the lower deck, even in winter, when it was freezing. Then she and her friends wore black duffle coats and breathed grey mist out of their mouths, pretending they were in Siberia. When the fog was thick, the sky ahead was bright white like a painted cloud and you could see nothing at all, so you might as well be anywhere, although perhaps not Siberia. The ferry would come to a stop and drift in the strange light, blowing its horn and sounding like a lonely elephant that had lost its herd. Then all the children on board would relax and start talking loudly and run up and down the decks, knowing they would be legitimately late for school.

Geraldine tried to catch Ezra that morning on the gang-plank when they arrived at Circular Quay, but he refused to acknowledge her, stalking off through the turnstiles, lugging his scratched black school bag. As much as anyone as small and thin as Ezra could be said to stalk, that is. Geraldine's mother always said how it tore her heartstrings to see little Ezra struggle off in the morning with that great black bag. But Geraldine was not deceived by his size. She knew there was nothing pathetic about Ezra.

She didn't catch him on the way home from school that afternoon either, as she had to stay late for a recorder practice. They were preparing for a performance at some unspecified (and possibly unwelcome?) date in the future – a piece called 'Schwanda the Bagpipe Player'. They'd been practising for so long now that they all knew their parts as well as their times tables, which took some of the gusto out of their playing, and the tune had developed a rather dirge-like drag to it.

Alma usually played the triangle at these rehearsals, pinging erratically at every fourth or fifth bar – their teacher was never sure which – but of course, she was not there that day. Far, far away, thought Geraldine, bitterly. Where had she gone – Finland? The Galapagos Islands? As she blew air through her recorder, Geraldine wondered if she could try the same strategy as Alma and off-load Alberta onto someone else – and who knows, maybe even Milly and Martha at the same time? Someone who might want guinea-pigs – there must be such people.

The late ferry that afternoon didn't get her home until just on six o'clock. It was already dark as she stepped off the connecting bus and turned down the street leading to her home. She pushed open the front wooden gate and banged her way into the living-room.

She heard with a shock the sound of her mother crying and she felt sick in the stomach. Parents didn't cry – that was something you grew out of, like wearing nappies. She walked slowly through the hall and peered around the corner.

Her mother was sitting alone at the dining-room table, her face in her hands, elbows resting on the long white pages spread out before her.

'Mum?' said Geraldine. 'Are you all right?'

'No,' said Geraldine's mother, not looking up.

Geraldine hesitated, then turned around and ran down to Violetta's room. Violetta was bent over her desk with a cassette recorder, playing a French tape.

'What's wrong with Mum?' said Geraldine, coming up from behind.

Violetta jumped. 'Don't sneak up on me like that, Gerry!'

'What's wrong with Mum?' Geraldine repeated. 'She's crying.'

Violetta sighed and twisted round on her chair. She pressed the pause button on the recorder.

'You know, Geraldine. Dad's business.'

'But why is she crying like that? Where's Dad?'

'He went to the doctor,' replied Violetta. 'About half-an-hour ago.'

'What's wrong with him?'

Violetta released the pause button. *'Il voudrait mieux de ne pas aller au manifestation avec Luc,'* advised the machine.

'I don't know,' said Violetta. 'He's got a pain in his stomach, or something.'

'Since when?'

'*Parce-qu'il n'est jamais bien habillé,*' replied Violetta, staring down at the table like her mother, shoulders hunched. She had a very nice accent.

Geraldine walked quickly out of Violetta's room to her own and flopped down face-forward on the bed. Her room was grey and dark in the dusk.

She sat up and looked out the window. Across the fence she saw the lights on in Ezra's house and heard the faint sound of television. She wondered what they were watching – probably something solemn and dull, like the news or today's parliamentary highlights. She flopped back down on the bed.

She hoped there was nothing too wrong with her father. Apart from going bankrupt, of course, and there wasn't much a doctor could do for that. What would happen to them all, she wondered. Would they have to go and live in Brazil, and move house every six months, pursued by heartless creditors?

She could hear the pigs squeaking, mewling, wanting their evening pellets. Tears came unaccountably into her eyes at the thought of them. Poor hungry little things. Why should they be so afraid of her? Why couldn't they love her, just a little bit?

Well, she had to feed them some time. Alberta

43

was so big, who knows what she might be driven to if her dinner were delayed – she might start eating the cage. Geraldine dragged her feet past Violetta's room out to the laundry, stepping over a basket of clothes, and picking up a handful of raisins from a bowl on the kitchen bench on her way past. She took a separate handful of pellets from the container in the laundry and trod out across the dry yellow lawn to their cage.

'Dinner time!' she said brightly, then stopped still. The cage door was open. She'd forgotten again. Not that it mattered much, except for the danger of a local cat leaping in and attacking them. She'd have to be more careful – Alma would not appreciate a mangled Alberta.

She bent over and started shaking down the pellets, like manna from heaven, she thought with a sigh. The pigs were under the blanket. It was really getting so smelly and threadbare – she knew she should replace it, or wash it at least. Imagine all the diseases that could be breeding there.

The unappetising grey pellets fell to rest on the chicken-wire, rolling a little here and there. Perhaps not all that much like manna from heaven. She wondered how they had all got on together – at least so far there were no overt signs of a personality clash. The pet books claimed every guinea-pig had its own distinct personality, although she'd found it hard to ever tell any difference between Milly and Martha. Still, no one

44

was sulking in the corner, feeling left out, and there were no loose bits of fur from fighting.

She took hold of one moist corner of the blanket and gave it a shake. Out dashed Milly. She shook it again. Out scrambled Martha, instantly at Milly's side. She lifted the blanket right out in the air, like a nervous magician, unsure of what she was about to reveal.

'Alberta?' she said.

There was nothing there.

Geraldine stared. It was not one of those situations when you lose something and you can keep on searching over and over through all your drawers in case you overlooked it the first time. There was nothing to overlook here. There was Milly, there was Martha and there were the guinea-pig pellets. There was no Alberta.

She was gone.

It was not possible. Where could she have gone? There was no hole in the cage, no gap in the wire. The only points of exit were the cupboard doors on the top. Surely no guinea-pig, even one the unusual size and strength of Alberta, could have stretched up on her hind legs and heaved herself out the open door with her shoulders. What terrible necessity could have inspired such super-porcine feats of strength and cunning? Had poor Alberta understood what Alma had said about her father and the brown-paper bag? But Geraldine reprimanded herself.

As if a guinea-pig could understand English . . .

Milly and Martha sat panting in the corner, eyeing the pellets. Geraldine looked at them, with a sudden suspicion. They couldn't have. Couldn't have. Could they? It'll end in cannibalism, Ezra had said. But that was just Ezra carrying on. Milly and Martha couldn't possibly have eaten Alberta, no matter how hungry they were. All right, she was late that morning, and hadn't had time to give them their usual lettuce and carrot, but she still couldn't believe they could have swallowed a fellow pig twice their size. Although there was that snake she'd read about in India that swallowed a fourteen-year-old boy. But it was ridiculous. It was just Ezra carrying on. Honestly. Cannibalism. That Ezra . . .

Ezra!

The word spun in her head with the speed and venom of a bullet. Of course – that was it. Ezra. Who else? She might have known. It must be. Ezra. He'd crawled over the fence knowing she'd be late back from school, and liberated Alberta, without the slightest compunction. He'd let her go, just like that. Not thinking for a moment of Geraldine, of Alma, or even of Alberta herself.

Because how would poor Alberta cope in the wild suburban streets, with cars, cats and garbage trucks? Not to mention roller-blades and swimming pools, and poisonous snail baits. She wouldn't last a minute, the poor little (biggish) thing. In her rage, Geraldine managed to endow the redoubtable Alberta with the meekest and most unassuming of personalities.

Geraldine felt a kind of thoughtless fury with Ezra as if someone were doing a scribble pattern in her head. She gazed over the fence through the dusk at Ezra's house. Somehow she didn't have the power in her to confront him just now. She could imagine his cold ruthless responses, completely without regret for his actions.

She stood in the darkening garden, enraged. Milly and Martha were squeaking softly now, like dinner conversation. Perhaps they were discussing Alberta, and what had happened to their brief and robust visitor, wondering where she was. That makes three of us, thought Geraldine.

A shrug of night wind moved the hanging branches of the lemon tree. Beneath the round black tyre-swing, something stirred. A break in the dark. A flash of white.

But Geraldine was angry and saw nothing. She tossed her head back like a horse refusing a fence, turned around and stomped indoors.

6

Something White

Violetta's mother told her that their father had an ulcer, which is something you get from worrying too much. It meant he had to calm down and be very careful about what he ate, how much he ate and what time he ate it. The doctor had supplied him with quite a complicated diet printed on official-looking yellow cards. If you get ulcers from worrying, thought Violetta, it wouldn't be long before the rest of them got one as well, from worrying about her father's.

But there's no time, Violetta roused on herself, to waste on worrying. An ulcer is not too serious, after all, with the proper treatment. Her father simply had to be sensible and cautious. She sighed. It might not be so easy.

Violetta was almost always late coming home after school. She was so brainy, there wasn't enough time in the ordinary school day to fit in all her lessons, so frequently she had to stay behind afterwards. She didn't mind; in fact she liked it. The classrooms echoed, the playground was empty, the only sounds were of teachers starting up their cars or music groups practising in the hall. There were scarcely any school children on the late ferry, and she sat on the deck watching the sun set, red and yellow, over the harbour.

The day after they found out her father had an ulcer, Violetta came home just before six o'clock. Neither her mother nor Geraldine were visible anywhere, although some glutinous-smelling pulse was boiling on the stove – this was something recommended on the doctor's yellow program. Violetta sat straight-backed on the sofa in the living-room, pulling at the long strands of her hair, listening to her father watch a portable television in his bedroom, wishing he would get up and come and talk to her. Minutes passed, nothing happened. I could knock at the door, thought Violetta, but she didn't. She got up and poured herself a glass of home-made lemonade and went to her room to study.

As she eased down her heavy school bag, it occurred to her that she should not have told Geraldine that they were going bankrupt. Her parents had not told her – it had required several nights of concentrated eavesdropping for her to find out, to paste the clues together, to convince herself that what they were saying was true. The business had failed, and it would not recover. Their house was going on the market. Everything was going to change. She shouldn't have told Geraldine, and frightened her like that. Her mother would be cross.

Violetta bent over her desk and gave her head a shake. She took a deep sip of sour, bracing lemonade, and at once felt better, for a moment at least. It wasn't so bad. That's why her parents hadn't told her what was happening. It wasn't such a serious thing. People were always going bankrupt. It wasn't so unusual or terrible, was it? Why, some people do it again and again and again. The thought made her hands tremble and she had to put the glass down or she would spill it. She couldn't stand it to happen again. That would not happen to them – no, never – their mother would not allow it. This would be their only disaster, she was sure. They would move house, her father would get better, her mother would get a promotion and everything would be fine.

She pulled over her sweet-smelling, thick-paged physics textbook. Concentrate on the really important things, she told herself. Things that will last. Not the trivial little annoyances of everyday life . . .

Unaccountably, this thought brought to mind

not the admirable laws of thermodynamics, but her boyfriend, Marcus. And as often happened when she remembered Marcus, Violetta sighed.

Marcus was the same age as Violetta and he had been her boyfriend for about six months. He was also full of brains – he and Violetta had met at an inter-school maths meeting for brainy people at the beginning of the year. Violetta found herself rather overpowered by Marcus. Not by his brains, which were considerable, but hers were equally so. It was his conversation. There was only one thing that interested him, and that was Africa.

Marcus was mad about Africa. Every aspect of Africa. Really, thought Violetta, if he had to have a place to be mad about, couldn't he have picked Greenland or Antarctica? Africa had so many countries, so many people, so many animals, so many wars, so many languages, so many varieties of national dress. So much of everything to learn about and remember. And the thing about Marcus was, he expected her to be as interested as he was – he thought it was only natural.

Marcus had a lot of African friends. In fact, apart from her, he seemed to have only African friends. Until she had known Marcus, Violetta had to confess to never having met an African person in her life, but now she met them by the dozen. She mentioned this to Marcus, once, and he smiled in his very adult way.

'You had a rather closed social circle before you

met me, didn't you darling?' (He always called her darling, as if she were fifty, at least.)

Violetta felt like pointing out that you might just as well say that Marcus had a rather closed social circle himself, seeing the only people he ever saw were from Africa. They had rather lovely names, Violetta thought, Marcus's African friends. Like Oliver, and William. They shook her hands enthusiastically and smiled kindly at her, but they always made her feel so weak and pale and small and somehow insignificant. Perhaps it had something to do with size – African people, well, the ones Marcus knew, seemed enormous.

She also found their accents difficult to understand – Violetta was used to the Hungarian accent of the grandmother of one of her school friends, but there appeared to be little relation between say, Ghanian, and Hungarian accents, which was not perhaps surprising. With Marcus's African friends she had to adopt various ruses, the alternate 'oh' and 'hmmm' and the occasional, more risky 'that's great', quickly turned into a 'I mean, how terrible', if it was returned with an uncomprehending frown.

If she went to a film with Marcus, it was an African film. If they listened to music, it was African music. If they went to a restaurant, it was African. She found herself looking at Marcus out of the corner of her eye sometimes – could he be a little unbalanced? Certainly his parents were strange people, and they do say if you have strange parents, you can end up a bit odd yourself.

She had only met his parents once, on a visit that Marcus had proposed one afternoon as they were sitting together in the front garden. Marcus had ridden over on his bicycle as usual, and had propped it up against the garden furniture. Violetta gazed down at the pebbled ground while Marcus read aloud excerpts from a magazine called New African Poetry. Violetta's mind was wandering, trying to surmise what the Old African Poetry might have been like, and whether it would have been more to her taste.

'So what do you say?'

Violetta jumped.

'Oh well . . .' she said. 'It's quite . . . '

'Just a cup of tea,' said Marcus with a frown.

'Oh, all right,' replied Violetta, relieved, although she would prefer lemonade. 'Shall we have it out here?'

Marcus frowned again. 'Not now, darling. I mean when you come and visit my parents.'

'Oh!' Somehow she didn't associate Marcus with parents. He seemed so very old. Even the first time she had seen him at the maths conference in his uniform, he had seemed aeons older than everyone else, including the teachers.

'They always want to meet my girlfriends,' Marcus went on, grandly, as if there had been a long string of girlfriends in the past, which Violetta frankly found hard to believe. Marcus was an acquired taste, like pickled eggplant or extra-dry vermouth. He would not appeal to every sixteen-year-old girl.

'That'll be great,' said Violetta, weakly.

'I'll meet you at the bus-stop then,' said Marcus. 'About four, all right?' And he bent his head back to the volume of New African Poetry.

So some days later, Marcus met her at the bus-stop, dressed rather more conservatively than usual, in black trousers and a white shirt. (At social occasions, Marcus often wore a traditional costume from Nigeria, which consisted of a long striped dress reaching to his ankles.)

'Just a few streets down,' he said, cheerfully striding ahead.

It was a wealthy-looking area, Violetta observed, high up on a hill with big white houses and views of the ocean. Marcus did not talk as they walked, concentrating on swinging to and fro the black umbrella which he always brought with him, and which Violetta had never actually seen him open. Which character was it in Batman that was always carrying an umbrella? The Penguin? Well, it was no use asking Marcus, as he never watched television, unless it was a documentary about Africa, of which there seemed to be a depressingly large number.

'This is it,' said Marcus, coming to a halt and pointing upwards with the umbrella's tip.

Violetta peered up. It was a large, two-storey

house, with a clean and spacious front lawn. Marcus opened the gate, and she followed him up the very thin paved path.

'I think we'll see Mother first,' said Marcus. 'Otherwise she might get difficult, you know.' He pulled out a bunch of gold-coloured keys from his pocket, and fitted one in the front door.

'Mother!' he called, as he swung the door open.

Marcus's mother was standing, rather disconcertingly, right on the doorstep. She was a short, middle-aged woman with long grey hair. She smiled very sweetly at Violetta but seemed to be at an utter loss as to what to say to her, or to her son, for that matter. Fortunately Marcus did most of the talking, as he probably had done for the past sixteen years. So they drank tea and ate orange-cream biscuits and listened to Marcus drone on. Violetta drank two cups, well-sugared, and found herself feeling quite relaxed with this quiet smiling woman who asked her no alarming questions.

'Well,' said Marcus eventually, finishing off the last biscuit. 'Better go up and see the old man, Mother. You know what he's like. Might get difficult.'

Marcus's mother looked at him politely, as if she had no idea at all, but didn't want to contradict him. Violetta shot a look at Marcus – what did he mean, go up?

'Lovely to meet you,' said Violetta, standing. 'Thank you for the tea.'

Marcus leant over and kissed his mother's cheek. 'I'll drop by later,' he said kindly.

Drop by? Didn't he live here? Violetta followed him out the front door, which he again locked with his gold-coloured key, and then up a side concrete stairway to the second floor of the house. Another key was produced, and a second door opened.

'Father!' called Marcus. He took Violetta's hand and led her in to a pale green room with a long-furred white carpet. 'My parents are divorced,' he mentioned casually. 'So separate quarters, naturally.'

'Naturally!' agreed Marcus's moustached father, stepping forward and heartily shaking her hand. 'Viola, how are you?'

'Violetta, Father,' said Marcus with a patient sigh. 'A viola is a musical instrument, close relative of the violin.'

Later, Marcus explained to Violetta that his parents had been divorced since he was five years old, but had chosen to go on living in the same house, his father upstairs, and his mother underneath. Marcus lived with his mother till he was eleven, then moved upstairs with his father – this had apparently been part of the divorce settlement. Marcus told her all this in such a worldly, matter-of-fact way, as if challenging her to suggest that this was not quite a common arrangement. And indeed, it might well be, for all Violetta knew. She could just imagine telling Geraldine about it, and Geraldine rolling her eyes and saying she knew thousands of people's parents who lived like that, and honestly, if Violetta would only get her eyes off her textbooks for half a moment . . .

She drank another two cups of well-sugared tea with Marcus's father, and two more orange-cream biscuits of the same brand. Did they do the shopping together, she wondered, pushing the trolley around the supermarket arguing over what to buy just like undivorced couples?

Except for the moustache, Marcus's father was astonishingly like Marcus. He had a different obsession, though, which was something of a relief, as two people raving on about Africa would have been hard to take. Marcus's father was interested in rudders. He had shelves of books about the history of the rudder throughout the house, and photographs of various rudders he had known through his long, apparently rudder-filled life. He had been to rudder museums all over the world, and even had a collection of pieces of celebrated rudders salvaged from wrecks in the South Seas and the Baltic, which were brought out and dutifully admired by Violetta.

Finally, at about half-past five, when it was already dark outside and Marcus's father was struggling to remember just where he had picked up an indeterminate scrap of black wood that he had gently placed in Violetta's hands like a live cockroach, Marcus stood up.

'Well, Father, time to go, I'd say.'

'Thank you for the lovely tea,' said Violetta, leaping to her feet, surreptitiously placing the piece of sacred rudder on a nearby bookshelf. She hoped Marcus would at least walk part of the way with her to the bus-stop, as she was not quite sure of the direction. But Marcus had strong ideas about female independence, which coincided most frequently with his own comfort. 'Just turn right at the second street,' he instructed her, as he saw her out with a shiver. 'It's cold tonight, isn't it, darling?'

Violetta took her seat on the bus, full of tea and sugar, her stomach sloshing like a samovar, and she watched the lights of the harbour on one side and houses on the other speed by. When she came home, she found her father sitting in the kitchen, plucking idly at his guitar, his hair falling over his face. He smiled at her, stopped playing, and took her hand. 'You're late, aren't you?' he said, tenderly.

Violetta sat down at the table next to him.

'My poor Violet,' said her father.

The sight of her father shot all thoughts of Marcus and his peculiar parents from her mind. She wanted to take him by the shoulder and shake him and say, 'What's going on, what are we going to do, what's happening? Are you going to get another job, start a new business, sell the house, have an operation, go overseas?' But, 'How's your ulcer?' was all she asked.

'Oh, all right,' he said, and ran his fingers up and down the neck of the guitar. He broke off, suddenly disenchanted. 'Oh God,' he said, and stood up and looked out the window to the garden.

The glass was dirty from grease and steam. There was something cooking on the stove – it smelt like cabbage. Cabbage and potatoes. One of the dishes her father had learnt to cook from his mother, and which seemed to have an inexhaustible sentimental attraction for him. You got used to the smell, Violetta supposed. She had got used to it herself. Perhaps when she grew up, she would find herself also yearning for these tasteless salty stews.

'Oh, Violetta!' her father whispered, though he was not looking at her. They had named her after a girl in an opera; someone sick, pale and passionate who comes to a sticky end. Violetta hoped she had too much intelligence to follow that path. She hoped, but she wasn't confident.

'Violetta!' He stiffened and grimaced. 'Come over here!'

Violetta went to stand next to him. 'What is it?'

Her father pressed his nose against the moist window, blocking out the reflection from the kitchen light with his hands.

'I saw something . . .' he said, squinting.

Violetta stared. He saw something? What did he mean, something? An intruder? A UFO? She waited for enlightenment.

'Something . . .' Her father's eyes were almost

bright, brighter than they'd been for days. 'Do you see anything?'

Violetta looked. The garden was black and bare – bare of anything out of the ordinary, that is. There was the lemon tree, the olive tree, the row of shrubs. There was Geraldine's tyre-swing hanging from its branch like a noose. There was the guinea-pig cage. Nothing else. Nothing that shouldn't be there.

'Nothing special,' she replied. 'I mean, what sort of thing are you talking about?'

'I'm not sure.' He let his hand drop and turned on his toes. 'Something . . . white.' He smiled down at her serious face. 'Very strange.'

Something white. Violetta was suddenly visited by the horrible fear that her father was having a nervous breakdown. Not that she knew what a nervous breakdown was, but she'd seen a man on television once, a man just like her father, about his age, with a wife and children, describing his nervous breakdown, and how he had started seeing and hearing things, and no one could get any sense out of him. What if that were happening to her father? He looked so odd, his eyes so suddenly alive. He saw something white?

Her father laughed, and sat down again at the kitchen table, taking up his guitar.

'I must be going mad,' he said, strumming again. 'Quite mad.'

7

Visitors

To Geraldine's relief, it seemed that none of her family had noticed the extra guinea-pig that had suddenly appeared and then so utterly disappeared. She had confronted Ezra about it at the bus-stop the next morning. Violetta, luckily, was not there, having gone in on the six-twenty for a before-school chemistry lesson.

Ezra denied everything. 'Don't be absurd,' he said, breathing out puffs of mist. 'Why would I do that? An animal like that couldn't survive out of captivity.'

Geraldine reflected that Ezra didn't know all that much about animals, whatever he'd read in books. A night's sleep was all she needed to remind her that one look at Alberta told anyone that an animal like her would survive anywhere, from the shrinking Sahara to the North Pole.

'Well, it's very strange,' she said, 'that she should disappear just the day after I showed you and you said all those awful things. She couldn't have got out by herself, you know.'

'She could, actually. You'd be surprised what an animal can do when it wants to,' Ezra replied firmly, looking down the street, hoping to see the bus. 'She probably crawled her way up the wire and out the open door. You left it open, you know.' He paused. Geraldine would not look at him.

'So what are you going to tell your friend?' he said, nastily.

'I don't know,' she muttered. 'I could say she died, I suppose. But she'd probably want to see the body. Or want a lock of her hair or something. I don't know.'

The bus appeared, wheezing and rattling as the door swung open. Geraldine stepped up inside, very low at heart. Perhaps he really hadn't let Alberta out. She almost believed him. Alberta had climbed out the open door. It was her fault. He was right. How on earth was she going to break the news to Alma?

She wished she could talk to her mother about it. Maybe she could think up a way of luring Alberta back inside the cage. Her mother was so clever, like Violetta. She taught philosophy at the university. Geraldine had always imagined the study of philosophy to be a peaceful, almost soporific business, involving a lot of sitting in a garden and staring at the sky while terrifying cosmic thoughts formed themselves in your head. Rather like being a nun, she had thought. But perhaps she was wrong about nuns, too, because her mother was anything but peaceful. She was always zooming off to the library or a tutorial or a wine-and-cheese night or to a lecture or to write an article. She had fair fluffy hair, and was full of schemes and ideas and solutions to just about everything. Her mother would have been able to think of something.

But that was before. That was how her mother used to be. Her mother had changed since their father's problems began. She still zoomed about, but she was different. She'd started to braid her hair into a tight plait with a rubber band at the end and now when she spoke it was largely practical matters that seemed to slip out of her mouth automatically, about clean shirts or how much milk was left in the fridge and would she mind running to the shop to get some more? She was always worried, thinking about something else, sitting and staring at pieces of paper with numbers all over them.

Even so, Geraldine might have told her mother. She might have caught her watering the garden one night, or waiting for the kettle to boil. While she was standing still, perhaps she could have told her. But then, that Saturday they had a visitor. And after that particular visitor, Geraldine lost all courage to tell anyone anything.

* * *

Visitors were not as unusual at Geraldine's house as at Ezra's, but this one was. He arrived in a light-green limousine, with a chauffeur who stayed in the car outside reading the newspaper.

'Look at that car!' said Violetta to Geraldine as they came home from their usual Saturday trip to the local library. 'Like a wedding.'

A pretty revolting wedding, thought Geraldine scornfully as she followed Violetta indoors, but was quickly distracted by her surroundings. While they'd been out, their parents had been cleaning the house. All the stray bits of paper and toys had disappeared, and the crimson walls of the living-room gleamed as if they had been polished. But no one polishes walls, thought Geraldine. Do they? Perhaps it was one of those mysterious tasks people's mothers find themselves doing in moments of deepest despair, like ironing sheets.

'I wonder what happened to all the toys,' Geraldine said to Violetta. 'It doesn't seem like our house without the toys.'

She found out when she went to put her books in her room. There were the toys – all of them. On her bookshelves, her chest of drawers, her desk.

Her parents must have thrust them there in their hurry to clean up, like sweeping dirt under the carpet. They huddled together, like in pictures she'd seen of refugees from war, staring at her with dead hopeless eyes; a strange collection of dolls, soldiers, dogs and bears, and the occasional wind-up clown. She felt as if she were being assessed by them, even condemned, they sat so still and silent. She thought of throwing a blanket over them, but somehow it seemed wrong, like covering a dead body.

Geraldine left her room and found Violetta in the corridor, a finger to her lips. Their father was laughing in the living-room, but it didn't sound like a happy laugh. Violetta pushed Geraldine forward a little, and they moved tentatively together around the corner.

Their father, grinning, stood at the window, pointing at the backyard; their mother, not grinning, was leaning against one wall as if she were terribly tired. And their visitor, in a dark suit and with blue-rimmed glasses and a tumbler of alcohol in his hands, stood in the centre.

Neither Geraldine nor Violetta had ever seen him before. His hair was partly grey, partly brown, and he looked very rich. Geraldine's father was not poor – at least, she supposed, not until he became bankrupt – but he had never looked as rich as this man, who gave the impression of being the sort of person who would light his cigarettes with a roll of American hundred-dollar bills. Of course, the car outside added to his general mystique, but to Geraldine it was not really him, but how their parents were behaving that made this man's wealth obvious and somehow sinister. Her father, for all his laughter, seemed frightened. She was used to him being tired or sad or exuberant or irritating. She was not used to him being frightened.

'Girls!' he cried out with relief as he saw them. 'My daughters, Violetta and Geraldine.'

The visitor smiled non-committally. He was staring straight ahead, with a peculiarly concentrated focus, through his bright blue-rimmed glasses.

Violetta pulled Geraldine's sleeve. 'Let's get something to eat,' she murmured. She sensed that they were not welcome, and the man made her feel embarrassed. She longed for a cup of tea, to sit at her desk with a nice fat textbook, to make some comforting chemical calculations. She dragged an unwilling Geraldine, who had nothing comparable to attract her to her room and rarely suffered from social discomfort, into the kitchen.

'Who is he?' whispered Geraldine. 'He must be here to buy the house. Did Dad tell you?'

'Hmmm.' Violetta shrugged. She felt slightly sick. Her mother looked terrible – what was going on? She wanted to leave the house, to get away from that man, but she didn't want to desert her parents. Who was he?

'Look!' said Geraldine, pointing out the side window. 'Ezra's parents must be having a party.'

Violetta looked out. A party? Surely not. But cars were rolling up outside, and people heading up Ezra's front path to the open door. They didn't exactly look dressed for a party, and they were a rather odd collection in age and certainly in appearance, but they all seemed to know each other.

'Must be relatives,' was Violetta's verdict, pressing her face against the glass. But she quickly retreated when one of them, a boy about her age, noticed her interest and gave her a friendly wave as if to invite her in as well.

'Who was that?' asked Geraldine.

'I've no idea,' Violetta replied, but she thought the boy had a rather nice face.

*   *   *

Ezra's guests, of course, were not relatives at all, but members of Animal Liberation arriving for their monthly meeting. In the event, it proved impossible for Ezra's parents to 'keep out of the way', as his mother had suggested, because the members were desperately friendly and keen to make them join in and feel one of the gang.

Ezra's father escaped into the garden during the preliminary proceedings, only to be pursued by the two pale-haired elderly ladies who, as it turned out, were not terribly interested in the preliminary proceedings either. But they were very interested in Ezra's father's cactus garden and wandered about, poking back overgrown ferns and advising him on soil nutrients.

Then they discovered a large spider web, and Ezra's father happened to mention that he had a soft spot for spiders, and could never bear to kill them. Well, nothing could have been more endearing; they immediately felt he was a most humane friend of their bosom, and all sat themselves down on the rather tatty garden furniture for a 'good old chat'.

This meant that things inside, where Ezra's mother was trapped, went much more smoothly than usual, without interruptions and arguments. 'Business' was over and done with quickly, and after that, people felt somehow much more inclined to talk about nothing in particular than they normally were, while Ezra supplied cups of tea from their very large teapot, a rarely used gift from a rarely seen cousin. Ezra's mother made conversation.

'And what are you studying at the moment?' she asked Simon brightly, sitting on a stool as she handed him a cup. A fairly safe sort of question, one might have thought, but Simon began one of his long, long, distressed monologues about medieval Nordic languages that Ezra was so familiar with. Still, his mother didn't seem to mind – she made no attempt to escape, although that might have been the mesmeric effect of Simon's waterfall of words, like a mouse under the hypnotic stare of a snake.

In the end, when everyone else had sidled out, nodding and smiling, and got back into their cars or walked off towards the bus, Simon was still trying to explain himself to Ezra's mother, and continued to do so as she and Ezra cleared away the dishes and washed everything up. But, at last, while Ezra's mother was down on the kitchen floor sweeping up the pieces of a teacup that Simon had dropped while trying to balance it on top of another three, Simon suddenly looked stricken and said, 'What happened to my aunts?'

'Your aunts?' Ezra had never heard of Simon's aunts, let alone knew what had happened to them.

'You know,' said Simon, in a panic. 'Those two old ladies with the white hair that drive everybody crazy.'

'Oh!' They were Simon's aunts? 'I didn't know they were your aunts,' said Ezra.

'No, well, we don't look all that alike,' agreed Simon. 'They're my grandmother's sisters. But they always give me a lift home!'

'I think they're still out there talking to my husband,' said Ezra's mother, peering out the window.

Simon joined her at the window with a sigh of relief. 'Otherwise I'd have to get the bus,' he said.

Ezra wondered if his father might have fallen

asleep with his eyes open. He went out the back
door to have a closer look, followed by Simon.

'Thought you'd shot through, aunties!' said
Simon cheerfully, and Ezra's father jumped in his
seat. 'I've just been doing the washing up.'

'Is that so?' said one of the aunties, drily.

'We've been having a lovely chat out here,' said
the other aunty, giving Ezra's father's arm a little
pat. 'Why haven't you been bringing your father
to our meetings, Ezra?'

'Oh!' said Ezra in surprise. 'I never thought of it.'

Ezra's father gave him a look as if to say, 'Well,
don't start thinking about it,' and stood up, shaking
the splinters of the wooden chair from his trousers.
'It's getting late,' he mentioned meaningfully,
waving an arm in the general direction of the
sunset, which was spreading across Geraldine's
back lawn in a mysterious red glow. Simon's aunts
followed this gesture with their eyes.

'Just look at that citrus!' said one, eyeing the
lemon tree.

'The lawn's a little ragged, though, I must say,'
said the other. 'I mean, I know it's winter . . .'

'Oh!' Her sister shrieked – not dramatically, but
like someone stepping on something soft and wet
as they walk barefoot along the beach. 'What was
that?'

'What?' asked Simon, squinting forward.

'Did you see that . . . that . . ?' said his aunt.
'Over there, under the tree?'

Simon stepped across the back patio to the fence. 'What are you talking about?'

His aunt was staring fiercely into Geraldine's backyard, puzzled. 'It doesn't seem to be there now,' she muttered. 'But I'm sure I saw something. White. Peculiar,' she added, thinking about it.

'A cat?' suggested Ezra's father.

'Oh no, not a cat!' she said, almost contemptuous, but she covered it up with a sweet smile. 'If you'd seen it, you wouldn't think for a moment it was a cat. It was so big, for one thing. And it looked . . . well . . . almost feral, you know. Rather nasty. Like a rat.'

'Not that we divide animals into the nasty and nice, of course,' said her sister quickly. 'Just a manner of speaking, you know.' This was addressed to Ezra's father, who nodded without understanding. He was quite happy to divide animals into the nasty and nice.

'Where was it?' asked Ezra, stepping forward, curious. Simon's aunt pointed over to the tree where Geraldine's tyre swung, round and black, back and forward in the wind. The guinea-pig cage stood on one side, the quivering blue blanket just visible in the growing dark. Ezra frowned. He felt his shoulders jolt for a moment. Was that something? He focused more intently.

'I . . .' he said. 'Something white . . .'

'Yes!' Simon's aunt nodded encouragingly.

'That's just how I'd describe it. See! He saw it! Something white!'

'Well, that could be a paper bag,' Simon pointed out, rather peeved at being unable to make out anything himself.

'Could be one of the little girl's pets,' said Ezra's father. 'She's got guinea-pigs or something there, hasn't she?'

'My dear man,' replied Simon's aunt, 'if you'd seen what Ezra and I had seen,' and she put a proprietorial arm around Ezra's waist, 'you'd know that that creature could not possibly be a guinea-pig.'

'Anyway, we'd better be going.' Simon felt it was time to draw speculation to a close. 'I'll miss dinner.'

The place where Simon lived at the university served meals three times a day, like an orphanage, and Ezra had noticed before Simon's anxiety not to miss out on his allotted portion. Ezra pictured him rushing forward with his bowl at the very end of the queue, only to be greeted with an empty ladle by the fat cook standing behind the pot, licking his greasy lips.

Violetta, in the meantime, had come out onto the back verandah, finding it impossible to think properly with the stranger in the house, and her father's unsettlingly loud and hearty laugh booming out every few minutes. She had avoided the backyard since the coming of the pigs: the way they squeaked, the way they smelt, the way they scuttled. Every time she saw them, she started thinking of statistics relating to the bubonic plague. But restlessness drew her out.

She noticed Ezra and his guests standing by a tall, pear-shaped cactus covered in white fur that Violetta had always thought must have been a kind of fungoid disease. Ezra's father was a little odd, really – surely planting all those cactuses couldn't be normal. Flowers were one thing, even ferns, but those rows and rows of succulents, some of them disturbingly large . . .

The low window of the dining-room was suddenly pushed open. The voices of her father and his mysterious guest were carried out into the dusk.

'Great sunsets!' her father was declaring, and even this simple statement was accompanied by a laugh.

'My God!' came the unexpected reply. 'What was that?' The visitor's head poked out the window, the blue of his glasses glinting in the half-light. He put his foot up over the low window-sill and hopped out onto the grass. Violetta stared. The stranger looked so crisp and clean in his expensive suit and curving hair, standing there on her damaged, sloping back lawn. Violetta found her eyes focusing on his beautiful glossy shoes with shining buckles, and she remembered a line from a hymn they sang at school: 'How beautiful are their feet!'

'Just over here,' said the man in the blue glasses, gesturing towards the lemon tree.

'What?' asked Violetta's father, who had followed him out nervously.

Geraldine, attracted by the shouting, came out the back door. Ezra raised his eyes towards her, wordless.

'I don't know what it was.' Blue-glasses shook his head. 'Some sort of animal. White. This big,' and he moved his hands up and down like someone estimating the size of a fish.

'That's what I saw!' volunteered Simon's aunt with some excitement from over the fence. 'They tried to tell me it was a cat.'

The stranger looked nonplussed by the intrusion, but managed a brief smile of acknowledgement. 'This was not a cat,' he agreed definitely. 'This was more like a . . . I don't know . . . a rat.'

Geraldine frowned. Her father was briskly shepherding his visitor back into the dining-room, bribing him with the offer of another drink. Geraldine looked at Ezra, her throat drying.

'Funny, isn't it?' said Ezra's father. 'Must be some sort of optical illusion.'

'Well, not if you both saw it,' pointed out Simon. 'Maybe there really is something out there.'

'You can have collective illusions,' mentioned Ezra's father.

'Can you?' Simon raised his eyebrows. 'Even people who've never met each other?'

Ezra gestured at Geraldine to come down the other end of the fence. But she turned her back on him and ran down the side path. She would have gone on to the street, but the sight of the green limousine stopped her, and she stood trembling by the camellia tree under Violetta's window.

She knew what it was. What it had to be. Something white and violent in the garden. What else? Alberta. Alberta was not dead. She was out there, waiting. Waiting for her. Waiting to make trouble. Waiting for disaster, hovering like a vulture in the African desert. There was something bad about that guinea-pig, she had sensed it from the very first time she had looked into those acute, intelligent pink eyes.

The front door opened. Geraldine stiffened behind the tree. Her father was seeing his visitor out. They were murmuring like stage conspirators, too low for her to understand. They did not see her, but looked at the ground, and into each other's eyes, very briefly. They shook hands. Her father walked with the visitor to his car, which started up as though by remote control as they approached.

After the limousine had sped away, her father stood alone in the dark garden for a moment, his hands in his pockets. Geraldine remained quite still beneath the tree's branches, watching. Her father uttered a long sigh, like air oozing out of an inflatable toy. He took his hands out of his pockets, and hugged himself. The moon shone on the grass. He shook his head slightly and walked quickly inside the house, slamming the door behind him.

8

Strangers

Geraldine was nervous. Although nervous wasn't the right word – that's what you felt before an injection, or before you had to make a three-minute speech in front of the class on the life cycle of a tadpole. This was much worse.

She slept badly, dreaming about Alberta. She deliberately banished both Alma and her guinea-pig from her conscious daytime mind, only to have her come back at night: Alberta laying down the law about the dirty floor, her homework, her untidy uniform; Alberta sitting in the best chairs in the house, eating all the chocolate out of the fridge; Alberta even sleeping next to her in the bed, pushing her off the pillow. Biting her.

Sometimes Geraldine would wake with the pain

of those two front teeth around her finger, her heart beating in shock, sure she must have screamed out loud. Oh, thank God, thank God, thank God, she would whisper. There was no Alberta. She hadn't crept in through the window noiselessly, scampered over the floor to her bed to attack her. It was just a dream. Quite the silliest sort of dream. Still, she started locking her windows at night, and fastening blankets over them with drawing pins.

What was she going to do? How was she going to tell Alma? She couldn't imagine recapturing Alberta. How on earth would she do it? Stalk her all night and pounce with a net? Lay a trap of food? It was too ridiculous – like Coyote and Road Runner in those Sunday morning cartoons. Her adversary would never allow herself to be caught. She would always be one step ahead.

It was the same at home. Something was going on. They were plotting something, and it felt like something bad. Her father was acting in an extremely nonchalant manner, which seemed to Geraldine suspicious – she preferred him, or rather, trusted him more when he was morose. Of course she wanted to see him happy, but he had no reason to be happy. He should be depressed. Look at his situation – bankrupt, creditors everywhere, house on the market and no buyers. But he bounced about the house singing 'Jimmy Crack Corn and I Don't Care', and never catching her eye. His already-too-long hair began to grow over his eyes, and he became more remote, more disguised.

He was always on the telephone, like a teenage girl in an American movie. Getting calls, making calls, hanging up on people in anger, ringing them back and apologising. Tuning his guitar, going to the doctor, making cheese sandwiches. And then quite often he would go out in the car, with hardly a word of goodbye. She would hear him come back, very late at night. Even if she was asleep, which was rare lately, the smell of the exhaust would wake her up, and the sharp jerk of the handbrake.

Where did he go? she wondered. Why did her mother never go with him? Her mother sat by herself late at night in the dining-room, elbows resting on the table. Thinking, Geraldine supposed. Praying even. She seemed to be expecting something, waiting for the supervisor to call out 'Time's up! Pens down!' at the end of an exam.

'Geraldine?'

Geraldine jumped in her seat, as if she were on springs. Jelly beans, which she'd been eating from a glass resting on her lap, scattered all over the living-room floor. She'd been sitting there watching television since she'd got home from school. It was now nearly six o'clock.

'Sorry, Gerry,' said Violetta, leaning over to help her pick up the jelly beans. 'I didn't mean to startle you. I thought you saw me.'

Geraldine had seen Violetta come in, of course. She'd just been shocked by the sound of her voice. Nerves, thought Geraldine.

'What is it?'

All the jelly beans were now back in the glass, covered with little bits of carpet dust, and not looking especially delicious. She could always wash them, she supposed, but then the colour would run, and the crunchy coating would get soggy. She stared down at them, transfixed by her dilemma.

'I just asked if Mum or Dad had told you when they'd be back,' said Violetta, patiently.

'I didn't know they'd gone anywhere,' replied Geraldine, surprised. 'I thought Dad was in bed.'

'Well, they're not home,' said Violetta. 'And I was thinking of going out myself. I was going to meet Marcus in town.'

Marcus. The thought of Marcus almost made Geraldine feel normal again, and took her mind off the jelly beans. Imagine voluntarily meeting Marcus anywhere.

'He wants me to help him buy a present for his mother's birthday,' added Violetta. 'I don't know why he thinks I could be of any use. I hardly know her.'

'It's Mum's birthday soon, too,' said Geraldine, changing the channel with the remote-control switch.

'I know,' sighed Violetta. 'It's actually on the same day. Marcus was so excited when I told him.

He thinks it means we're made for each other.'

Oh yeah, thought Geraldine. 'Do you ever kiss him?' she asked absently, changing the channel again. Most of the programs at this time of day involved a lot of kissing, so it naturally came to mind.

'Well, not exactly.' Violetta sighed again, more deeply this time. 'He doesn't seem to want to.'

This did not surprise Geraldine. If anything, she was relieved.

'I won't be long,' said Violetta, getting up. 'I don't think so, anyway. Tell Mum and Dad where I've gone, won't you.'

Geraldine heard Violetta push their thick wooden front door shut after her. It always reminded her of a castle, their door, with its wide, impressive dark-brown beams, and its round black handle and circular knocker. She switched off the television and lay back on the sofa with a sigh, her blue stockinged, shoeless feet up on the arm-rest. She preferred to be alone. She could close her eyes, pull a cushion over her head and try to stop her brain from spinning. Strands of her mother's long fair hair were spread across the fabric of the sofa.

Stretching out her legs, Geraldine knocked a toy off the coffee-table in front of her. She leant down lazily to pick it up. It was a teddy that played the drums, the cymbals and a trumpet – a one-bear-band, she supposed you might call it. It was a wind-up toy – her father didn't like batteries or things that plugged in. He liked keys and clockwork mechanisms; things that you could take apart and fix with a screwdriver, without calling upon the higher powers of electricity or the microchip. She wound the bear up and set it on the table, watching it wiggle from side to side as it belted out Brahms' Lullaby.

When it stopped, she wound it up again. And again. And again. It was surprising, really, that she heard the knock at the door at all. But it was a remarkably loud knock. Firm and determined.

She should not, of course, have opened the door, being alone in the house. These were her parents' repeated instructions. But, Geraldine objected, what if whoever knocked tried one of the side doors which were always unlocked, and actually came into the house and found her sitting there, frozen still, as if no one were at home? Or what if it were robbers, just knocking to make sure the house was empty before breaking in and then when they found her they'd murder her?

In any case, either because she was feeling nervous in general, or because her mother had forgotten to remind her not to open the door, had not even told her she was going out, Geraldine automatically got up from the sofa and went to open it. She switched the silver lock and tugged the door back over the carpet.

Two men stood there, one standing slightly

behind the other. The one in front spoke first.

'Hello there! Dad home?' Geraldine noticed their dark grey suits and their brown shoes. She shook her head.

'Mum?'

Geraldine noticed their blue shirts, their clean-shaven cheeks. 'Just me,' she said.

'Just you,' repeated the man.

'Any idea when they'll be back?' said the other man, smiling at her, rather kindly, she thought.

'I don't know,' said Geraldine. 'I don't know where they went.'

'Go together, did they?' asked the second man, but the first one made a cautioning gesture to him with his hand.

Geraldine shrugged. 'I don't know,' she said.

The two men looked at each other. 'Right then,' said the first one. 'We might come back another time.'

They started to back out, away from her, still smiling. Geraldine frowned. Perhaps she should ask if they had a message, or what they wanted, but some instinct stopped her. Some feeling that she would prefer not to know.

The front gate clicked shut, and Geraldine stood still in the doorway. She could not see past the fence from where she stood, but she could hear them, talking and opening their car door. She waited to hear them start up the engine and drive away, but nothing happened. There was no grinding of the ignition, no changing of gears like the drawing in of a painful breath as the car pulled away. Not a sound.

They weren't going anywhere, it seemed. Were they going to sit out there and wait until her father and mother came home? Didn't they believe her? Maybe they were just looking at a map, smoking a cigarette, trying to fasten a stiff seat-belt. Or were they waiting to hear her close the door, just as she was waiting for them to leave? Geraldine felt faint and cold.

Suddenly she jumped, for at least the second time that day. She saw Ezra, sitting on the step of his own front garden, looking over at her curiously. It was like seeing a painting suddenly wink at you, or a statue move its hand. She felt as white as he looked. Ordinarily, she might make a face at him, turn around and slam the door, but something in his dark eyes, some trace of unexpected sympathy, stopped her. She had scarcely spoken to him since the guinea-pig incident, but now she stood at the open door and willed him to say something.

He was eating an orange, very carefully, without spilling a drop of juice. He swallowed a segment, and mouthed at her as if to say, 'Who are they?'

Geraldine shrugged. She walked over to the wire barrier between the two houses.

'They want my mum and dad,' she said. 'But they're out.'

Ezra ate another segment of orange, spitting the pips carefully into his hand, as if they were the tiny eggs of some precious animal. 'I've seen them before,' he said.

Geraldine grimaced. 'Where?'

'At your house,' said Ezra. 'They knocked on the door but no one answered. Yesterday afternoon.'

Wednesday afternoon. Her recorder practice.

'Your parents were home, I think,' Ezra went on. 'But they didn't answer. Maybe you shouldn't have opened the door. Maybe your parents don't want to see them.'

'Oh maybe, maybe, maybe!' snapped Geraldine. 'You remind me of a . . . a tortoise!' she said ridiculously, but there was something in his long neck, his round eyes, his malevolent persistence.

'I don't see why,' replied Ezra calmly. 'I'm just telling you. Why don't you ask your mother?' He stood up, slipping the orange pips into his pocket. But she didn't want him to leave. She disliked him, but she didn't want him to go away.

'They're still out there,' she said, urgently. 'What do they want?' She couldn't bear to go back alone to that empty house, with those two suited strangers sitting outside. She turned to Ezra and said, 'Can I come over for a while?'

Ezra was taken aback, and unwilling, but, 'All right,' he said. 'If you want.'

Pulling herself over the fence, Geraldine followed him up the steps to his front door, half as solid as their own, and with no ornate door knocker, but it seemed to Geraldine she would be twice as secure behind it than at home. She looked back to glimpse the edge of the grey car parked next to the footpath. It sat there, like a dead spider on the laundry floor, motionless until someone bent down to sweep it away. She would stay at Ezra's until it was gone, she decided. Or until somebody else came home.

Simon

Violetta was spending a rather unsettling evening with Marcus in the bookshop. Of course, Marcus was never what you would call relaxing company, but in shops he was worse than ever. Violetta had a humble attitude to shopping. She would scurry in, peer furtively around for what she wanted, hurry over to pay for it and slip out as quickly as she could, hoping she hadn't caused anyone any trouble. But for Marcus, going shopping was one of life's great social adventures.

This was particularly trying to Violetta in a bookshop, which had for her some of the hallowed atmosphere of a library. Marcus had other ideas. They made their way out of the cold city down an escalator, into a big, modern bookshop, well-lit and brightly coloured.

'I'm looking for something on embroidered rugs,' he announced in such an enormous and forceful voice that several people lurking in the aisles of paperbacks glanced up in shock, as if he had demanded a pornographic magazine. Violetta was still in her school uniform, but Marcus had changed into a white shirt and black trousers, hitched up with bicycle clips, revealing orange socks. He might well look like the kind of person, thought Violetta, who has an unashamed interest in the seamier side of life.

'Embroidered rugs,' said the man behind the counter thoughtfully.

'Preferably eastern African,' Marcus continued. 'My mother has a particular interest in Kenyan handicrafts.'

This sounded most unlikely to Violetta, now she had met Marcus's mother. She more than suspected that Marcus was one of these people who buy presents for other people that they would like to receive themselves.

'Eastern African embroidered rugs,' muttered the man, obviously unwilling to admit they had no such thing.

'Or tribal music of Zimbabwe,' suggested Marcus, to show he was not being difficult.

The man nodded, a blond lock falling over his tortoise-shell glasses. 'Come this way,' he said, with a sudden and masterful gesture, walking briskly down to the back of the shop. 'There might be something here for you.'

It didn't take Violetta long to realise that this was going to be a prolonged evening, and one in which her advice was not going to be called upon with much frequency. Marcus was telling the man, whose name was Ted, according to the label on his red shirt, all about his long-term interest in African needlework, and how waterways of the Gobi desert was not quite the same thing. Ted was undaunted, however, and optimistically showed him a book on Egyptian cuisine, with the same admirable spirit as an estate agent who shows the client a two-storey shop with a spacious courtyard when what they asked for was a three-bedroom house with a lock-up garage.

'A beautifully presented book,' remarked Ted, flipping over the glossy food-filled pages.

'Ah, yes, the Moroccan influence ...' murmured Marcus non-committally, scanning the index at the back.

Why on earth did Marcus ask her to come? If he really wanted her advice, she would have suggested getting his mother some fragrant drawer liners, or even some crystallised ginger, of which she had noticed the older generation was peculiarly fond. That's what she was going to get her mother, anyway. Not that her mother was quite as old as Marcus's. You couldn't really compare the two at all, come to think of it, apart from the fact they were both mothers. But that must be bond enough, surely.

Ted and Marcus had somehow gotten onto the subject of the spawning of tree frogs, and Violetta found herself wandering away. The shop was long and deep, with cards hanging above the aisles to tell you what category you were in, like in the supermarket, although instead of 'Baking goods', 'Deodorants', and 'Confectionery', there was 'Australiana', 'Horror', and 'Sociology'. Violetta came to a stop in the 'Humour' section. She looked along the row at the various books designed to make you laugh, with pictures of people sitting on toilets or cats hanging upside-down from rafters. Then she noticed with a frown several copies of a sombre edition of *On the Origin of Species*. Surely that must be a mistake, unless . . .

'Hello, there!'

She swung around, her hand dropping down from the book. A man – well, a boy, really – stood there smiling at her. He was wearing jeans and a T-shirt with a slogan on it, and he seemed somehow familiar.

'Hello,' she replied. Perhaps he didn't look familiar, perhaps he was a salesperson, or a Mormon.

'You live next door to Ezra Perlman, don't you?'

Ezra Perlman. She had never known Ezra's last name. It was rather beautiful, and suited that silent, oyster-like family.

'Yes . . .' she began, thinking. It was not difficult now to make the connection – she and Ezra had very few things in common. 'You were there last weekend, weren't you? At Ezra's? With all those people.'

This was the boy who had waved at her, as she had stared at him through the kitchen window.

'Yes.' Simon held out his hand to be shaken. 'Simon.'

Violetta took it. 'Violetta,' she said.

'I thought you might be coming in to the meeting,' said Simon.

'Oh well.' Violetta was not actually sure what the meeting had been about.

'Are you interested in Animal Liberation?'

'Oh well,' Violetta repeated, nonplussed, and added truthfully, 'I suppose I'm interested in most things.' Except eastern African embroidery, she thought with a disloyal pang.

'Have you read this?' said Simon, pointing at *On the Origin of Species*.

'Well, parts,' replied Violetta cautiously. Perhaps he was a Mormon, after all, as well as an Animal Liberationist. And what did Animal Liberationists think about evolution anyway? They might have some extreme theory that showed it all to be a human conspiracy against the so-called lower orders of life. She did not especially want to get into that kind of conversation.

'I'm studying Scandinavian languages, actually,'

said Simon, as if this were somehow obscurely relevant.

'That sounds very clever,' suggested Violetta, relieved to abandon the question of evolution, but Simon grinned at her, rather endearingly.

'Well, I'm not much of a student, you know,' he confessed. 'Not much concentration. I should give it up, really. But I suppose once you start these things, you just have to keep going.'

Violetta did not suppose so at all. It seemed to her a very unsatisfactory way of running your life – the sort of thing that Geraldine might say. 'Well, I do think,' she said, 'you should be able to know when you've made a mistake and do something about it.'

'Violetta!'

Marcus's voice boomed out. Violetta jumped. 'Oh, I better go. It's my friend.'

Simon nodded, looking at her thoughtfully. 'Well, see you later,' he said.

'Okay.'

'Maybe at Ezra's place.'

Violetta nodded, smiling politely. She wondered, as she turned down the middle aisle of the shop, why she hadn't called Marcus her 'boyfriend'. And why she hadn't offered to introduce them. Marcus stood at the cash register with Ted, three expensive-looking books on the bench. He smiled at her.

'Meet someone you know?' he asked, sounding like an indulgent uncle.

'Well, sort of . . . ' she began, looking back down towards the 'Humour' aisle. Perhaps she should introduce them after all . . .

But Simon had disappeared. The aisle was empty. Violetta was not to know, but he had gone to find a public telephone.

10

Sisters

Inside Ezra's house, his father was watching television, while his mother was frying onions. The room felt comforting, warm and low-ceilinged. Ezra's father stood up in surprise when Geraldine and Ezra came in, pressing the 'mute' button on the remote control.

'It's Geraldine,' said Ezra. 'You know, from next door.'

'Of course I know Geraldine,' said Ezra's father heartily, as if they had an intimate acquaintance, rather than the occasional nod or good morning when their paths were forced to cross. 'Come over to play, have you?'

Ezra rolled his eyes. It made them sound about eight years old. Geraldine, frightened that Ezra would mention the two men in the car outside, said quickly, 'Yeah. Ezra's going to show me some books.' Ezra must have a lot of books, being such an egghead. That was a safe thing to say.

Ezra's mother came out of the kitchen, smiling. 'Hello, dear,' she said to Geraldine, but her gentle brown eyes were focused on her son. The onion crackled unseen in the kitchen, popping and spitting like an experiment in a scientific laboratory.

'Geraldine's parents have gone out,' Ezra explained.

'Oh dear,' said Ezra's mother. 'All night?'

Geraldine shrugged.

'What will you do for dinner?' asked Ezra's mother, for she was the sort of person for whom a meal was as important as a prayer.

'Oh, I'll find something,' said Geraldine, beginning to see pathos in her situation, quite removed from the two strangers outside. 'My sister's gone out too. With her boyfriend,' she added, to make her sound even more neglected. Ezra's parents would probably think Violetta had gone gadding off to a glamorous nightclub with some gorgeous man in a red sports car, to eat lobster and strawberry ice-cream, while her little sister chewed on cold peanut-butter toast at home.

'Well, I hope she's got a helmet,' was all Ezra's mother said, rather obscurely, but she had noticed Marcus from time to time dropping in on his bicycle, and she imagined Violetta somehow perched on the back of it.

'Have dinner with us,' said Ezra's father, unexpectedly, to Ezra at any rate.

'Yes, you must,' agreed his mother. 'That is, if you don't think your parents will mind.'

The state Geraldine's parents were in at the moment, she couldn't imagine them minding anything she did, if they even noticed. She wondered if Ezra and his family knew about what had happened to them, and how her father had gone bankrupt. Was this the sort of thing neighbours knew? In movies, neighbours either knew everything, standing at the window with their binoculars, or absolutely nothing, not even noticing when six people were murdered right next door. What category did Ezra's parents fall into?

Ezra led her into his room. On the wall above his bed hung a placard – 'Would you take your child to an abattoir?' Geraldine dropped her eyes from it quickly, to a framed photograph on Ezra's desk.

'Who's that?' she said, pointing.

It was a photo of a little dark-haired, dark-eyed girl. She had on blue corduroy overalls, with a pink cloth hippo sewn on the front panel, and she had red, round, lovely cheeks.

'That's my sister, Tory,' said Ezra. 'She's dead.'

'Oh.' Geraldine felt sick. Dead?

Ezra sat down on his bed. 'Well? What do you want to do?'

Dead.

'I don't know,' she said. She looked like Ezra, a rounder, redder Ezra. This little dead sister.

'I've got some books about guinea-pigs,' he said, getting up and going over to one of the shelves. 'You might learn something.' He pulled out a book and gave it to her. It was clean and well kept, as she imagined all Ezra's books would be. She looked down at the crisp, cool page. 'The guinea-pig is a chunky, furry animal with a benign but timid disposition,' she read.

Dead.

Ezra said something, but his voice sounded muffled, as if he were speaking underwater. Her heart, her mind, fell still. Dead.

'Ezra!' His mother called out from the kitchen. 'It's Simon on the phone again!'

Ezra left the room, but she hardly noticed. Dead.

When they sat down for dinner, she was placed between Ezra and his father. They had fried potatoes, fried onions and fried chicken schnitzel, with a free-range omelette for Ezra. Ezra's parents drank wine, while she and Ezra drank blackcurrant juice.

'So, what did Simon want?' asked Ezra's father, pouring Worcestershire sauce all over his meal. It looked like melted chocolate.

'He wants to drop round after school some time,' replied Ezra, sounding puzzled. 'A few things he wants to discuss, he said.'

'He's not bringing his aunts, is he?' Ezra's father

looked suddenly alarmed. 'By any chance?'

'Well, he didn't say,' said Ezra.

There was an uneasy silence.

Geraldine noticed more photos of the dead child on the sideboard and the mantelpiece. Nothing to show what had happened to her, just what you might have if she were still alive. In none of them did she look older than two or three. That must have been when she died. When did it happen? Geraldine wondered. Why? Was she sick? Was she in hospital and did they shave off all her hair?

'Funny, wasn't it,' interrupted Ezra's father, making the fork jump in her hand, 'that thing they saw the other night in your backyard?'

'Thing?' gulped Geraldine. She looked at Ezra, but he was cutting potato with the concentrated precision of a great European chef.

'Some sort of animal, I think,' said Ezra's father. 'White, you know. Like a cat.'

'Perhaps it was a cat,' said Ezra's mother, in a voice that had made this suggestion before.

'It wasn't a cat,' said Ezra.

Ezra's mother got up and went over to the front window of the living-room. She pulled the curtain aside a little.

'I'll tell you what's strange,' she said. 'There's been a car parked out there with two men inside it for hours now. Did you notice it, Geraldine?'

Geraldine put her knife and fork together in the

middle of the plate as she had been taught. She willed Ezra not to say anything.

'Anyway,' Ezra's mother continued, 'I think that's your sister coming in. Should you let her know where you are?'

Sister. Suddenly the word seemed vulnerable and very precious. Geraldine leapt gratefully to her feet. 'I'd better go,' she said quickly. 'Thank you for the lovely dinner.'

'You don't have to go right now!' protested Ezra's father. 'Stay and watch a movie. Have you ever seen *Paint Your Wagon?*'

'Well, no,' confessed Geraldine, and her eye caught the photo of the little girl, smiling into a great distance. *Paint Your Wagon*, whatever it was, might be more than she could take. She wanted to get inside her room, under her blankets. She wanted to listen to the radio through an earphone and close her eyes tight. 'I really better go.'

She scarcely acknowledged Ezra as she left the house, although he came out and watched her climb over the side wire fence. It was dark now, as dark as midnight, and the street lights were blazing. It was still there, that grey car. How long had it been now? Perhaps she should call the police. She could ask Violetta. She would know what to do.

Geraldine tossed her chin slightly at Ezra, which he accepted as a gesture of goodbye. He stood watching her, like a patient father, until she reached the door of her home and was safely inside.

11

Late At Night

'I had dinner at Ezra's,' said Geraldine, coming into the kitchen through the side door from the dark.

Violetta switched the electric kettle on to make herself a cup of tea. 'You shouldn't leave the house open like that,' she roused. 'Anyone might come in. I didn't know you were going out.'

'Well, I didn't know either,' said Geraldine. 'They just asked me all of a sudden.'

Violetta crouched down to look for a biscuit in the cupboard below the sink. 'Mum still not back,' she observed, finding an unopened packet of gingernuts. She straightened up.

'No.' Geraldine paused. She must tell Violetta about the two men. The two men still outside waiting in the car. They would have seen Violetta come in – maybe they thought she was her mother? It was dark, and they looked alike. Maybe they were coming to knock on the door again right now. But no, Violetta was in school uniform.

'I . . .' she began. 'There . . .'

'Mmmm?' Violetta looked up from pouring the boiling water over the tea-bag in her mug.

'Nothing,' said Geraldine. Nothing? Why nothing? What was wrong with her? Why didn't she say something? Why keep it a secret?

'Ezra's sister died,' she found herself saying, in a rush.

'What?' Violetta stared at her. 'Ezra? Ezra Perlman?'

'How do you know his surname?' asked Geraldine, diverted for a moment.

'Oh, I know lots of things,' replied Violetta complacently, dipping the round hard biscuit into her sweet black tea. It was true, after all, she did know a lot of things other people didn't.

'Well, she died,' said Geraldine. 'He showed me a photo of her.'

'Are you sure?' Geraldine was always getting things the wrong way round. 'Maybe you didn't understand him properly.'

Geraldine shrugged. She knew she had understood him. He could hardly have been more explicit. But she didn't want to talk about it. Any more than she wanted to talk about the two men in the car outside. She shivered.

Violetta looked at her with some concern. Gerry had really been very odd lately. So nervy. Ezra with a dead sister? It was possible, of course. But they would have heard about it before now, surely. Simon might know, she found herself thinking. Simon.

'Are you okay?' she said to Geraldine. 'You look so pale.'

Geraldine looked more yellow than pale, but it was the sort of thing their mother said when she was worried about them, hoping it might spur them on to further revelations as to why they looked so pale. But Geraldine only scowled.

'I'm going to bed,' she said.

* * *

By the time her parents came home that night, Violetta was sitting at her desk, studying ionic bonding and sucking the ends of her hair. She heard the sound of her father's car in the distance – the sound of a familiar car can be as distinctive and unmistakable as that of a familiar walk, or even a voice. She looked out the window of her room and could see easily over the front fence to the street junction where the car would turn and pull into their garage. But it didn't happen.

It was their car – she was sure of that, although it was almost midnight and the street light was flickering. It was their car's sound, and their car's colour, and it had her father and mother, shadowy, but themselves, sitting in it. But as it slowed down at the junction, ready to turn, it suddenly swung back to the main road, sped up and drove away again. That was odd enough – although she supposed they must have remembered they wanted to buy some milk or post a letter, and had rushed off to do it before coming home.

But then Violetta noticed the other car, the grey car that had been waiting all night in the street like a sleek, predatory cat, the car she had ignored as she came home, her thoughts full of Marcus and Animal Liberation. But now it shone its deep-reaching lights up the crest of the hill, filling the small space with bright whiteness, and the engine turned on. Then it, too, sped up and disappeared around the corner of the main road.

She felt uneasy. It reminded her of movies about World War II, and people escaping from prisoner-of-war camps, and Nazis in hard round helmets with flashlights and huge, wolf-like dogs gnashing their teeth at the shaking trees. She bent her head over her book. Her eyes were sore and she was tired, and thought enviously of Geraldine snoring peacefully in the room next door. Oh, to be that age, she said to herself; not a care, not a worry. Just to feed your guinea-pigs, play with your friends, and eat your dinner. Of course, Violetta had already forgotten what it was like to be Geraldine's age.

It was over twenty minutes later – Violetta kept looking at her watch – before her parents' car approached the corner again, but this time they turned and pulled into the garage as they should. She softly closed her chemistry book and waited, listening.

'Okay!' she heard her father say as he slammed the garage door, probably waking the neighbours up with the bang. They were murmuring as they came in the front door – her mother even laughed, although perhaps it was a rather bitter laugh.

Violetta got up from her desk and went down the corridor. She crouched against the wall in the darkness, listening. The hall door was slightly ajar, and she could just see into the living-room where her parents were sitting. Her father no longer drank alcohol, because of his ulcer, but her mother was drinking a beer from a short square glass. 'Perhaps it won't make any real difference,' she was saying, in the voice of a person who wants desperately to be contradicted.

'It'll make a difference,' said Violetta's father, sounding at the same time firm and uncertain. 'It must.'

'So what are you going to do?' sighed her mother. 'I mean, where we'll go in the meantime, I don't know. What does it matter.'

Her voice dropped, and she rubbed her tired

eyes, shaking her head softly, fair strands of her hair falling in her face, while she brushed them back with her white fingers.

'We'll arrange something,' said her father, again a mixture of confidence and doubt. He picked up the toy bear on the coffee table and stroked its prickly head.

'What about the girls?' her mother asked. 'When shall we tell the girls?'

Her father was silent, apart from the air noisily pushing in and out his unhealthy battered body. He puffs and pants like an old man, thought Violetta.

'Straight away,' he said. 'It's settled, after all. And we'll have to make a move quickly. The sooner they know the better, really.'

She heard him get up, and swiftly as a spy Violetta scuttled back down the corridor to her room. She sat on the edge of her bed. He would come in, in a moment, to kiss her goodnight. He always did. No matter how late he was up, she was always up later.

Violetta waited for him to come. She waited, motionless, listening to the blood rushing about her body. She waited and waited, but he did not come.

• • •

Ezra was also up late that night, thinking about Tory. And about Geraldine.

He couldn't understand himself. He couldn't understand why he had told Geraldine about Tory. He had told no one else; no one at school, no one in Animal Liberation. Why had he told her? He could easily have said she was a cousin or something – what would Geraldine care? Why on earth had he told her the most secret thing in his life?

He didn't even like Geraldine, and he knew she didn't like him. She'd only asked to come over because of those two men in the car. They weren't friends, not at all. And she'd just sat there in his room, looking about her with that frightened, sulky expression on her face, and he'd gone and told her about Tory.

Now she would tell everyone, and all the world would know. Her sister, her parents, those other girls she sat with on the ferry. They would come after him, ask him questions, they would want to know everything. That's what people were like about death. They wanted to know.

Although Geraldine hadn't. She hadn't said a thing. She'd just gone white, and started reading a book about guinea-pigs. Even her freckles had faded. She was a strange-looking girl. How did someone grow up to look like that, Ezra wondered. What would Tory have looked like at Geraldine's age?

Tory. Every day he still thought about her, and he knew his parents did as well. Little, dead Tory.

* * *

Geraldine lay on her stomach in bed, dreaming of Alberta. Alberta was taking her to task about her poor ability as a tennis player – how weak her shots were, and how rarely her serve ever entered the right square. Geraldine tearfully defended herself, screaming, 'I don't care! It's not true! I hate you!' She shouted in her sleep, and those were the words she woke up with sounding in her ears.

She sat up in bed, shaking. Perhaps she was getting sick. But her nose was clear, her throat was soft, she had no temperature. She had sometimes envied her friends at school who came down with glandular fever, forced to spend half a term in bed at home. How peaceful that would be, lying under the covers, eating buttered toast cut into strips . . .

She leant over to her window and looked into the night. The sky was clear, but the air was arctic. She stared up at the stars for a moment, and the round flat grey-flecked moon. She wished she had been alive when the people had flown up and walked on the moon, even driven a jeep on it – she'd seen a picture in an encyclopaedia. She'd asked her mother about it, but 'Oh yes, 1968, was it, or 67?' was all she'd said, with little more interest than if Geraldine had asked her when Abraham Lincoln was born.

She laid her head sadly on the pillow. Geraldine loved the moon. She yearned for it, and felt a biting envy for those astronauts.

12

Good News?

Violetta saw neither of her parents the next morning – she stayed in bed as late as possible and then ran out quickly into the cold at the last moment. Geraldine was still asleep as she left, and was obviously going to miss the ferry. Normally their mother woke Geraldine up, or sometimes their father. Very occasionally Violetta might take it upon herself to rouse her little sister, but only if their mother asked her to specially. Otherwise she preferred not to get involved – Geraldine was so bad-tempered at half-past six.

Violetta had intended to buy herself a doughnut at Circular Quay for breakfast, but she now realised sitting at the bus-stop feeling her seven o'clock hunger and the light weight of her wallet, that she had run out of the house without any money. An empty stomach and an empty heart, she thought miserably.

She watched Ezra coming up the hill, lugging his bag, his grey school hat half-coming off his head. The sight of him reminded her instantly of Simon, the bright-eyed boy in the bookshop, and she brightened a little herself. It would be nice, she thought carefully, to see him again.

Ezra was relieved to see Violetta alone at the bus-stop. He didn't want to face Geraldine that morning, after last night. He crossed the road, upended his hard plastic school bag and sat himself down on it.

'Oh Ezra,' said Violetta, breaking their usual morning silence.

Ezra shook in his damp blazer, swinging his head around. Now it was coming. Geraldine had told her and she was going to cross-question him. Oh, I heard the sad news from Gerry, Ezra. How awful, how tragic. Poor Ezra. What happened? How old was she? Will you ever get over it? Is your mother going to have another baby? I'm so sorry . . .

'I met someone who knows you last night,' said Violetta. 'Simon?'

'Simon?'

'You know, from Animal Liberation. He went to your meeting.'

'Oh, Simon.'

Of course, Ezra only knew one Simon, so it had to be him, but still he found it hard to imagine a place or a circumstance under which his Simon and Violetta might meet. Ezra's view of the world was that after school or work, people went to their homes and ate dinner. This was despite all the evidence he had observed to the contrary, but Ezra's attitudes were not always as scientific as he might have liked them to be.

'In town, in a bookshop,' said Violetta, looking over her glasses at him. She was not reading this morning, but she felt uncomfortable without glasses. They protected her eyeballs from the cold, she told herself.

'Oh.'

Really, this boy was hopeless. Hadn't he any curiosity? Or, if not, any social graces? Couldn't he think of something to say? What did he and Gerry argue about all the time?

They heard the bus squeaking and puffing from the nearby hill, making its tortured way towards them. Violetta took off her glasses and slipped them into the soft crimson case she kept in her coat pocket. Ezra stood up from his school bag and tugged it from the ground.

'Actually, he rang me last night,' he revealed as the headlights of the bus came round through the fog.

'Did he?' Did he?

'He wants to come round, for a visit or

something,' muttered Ezra, losing interest in Simon as the long grey day loomed ahead of him.

Oh. Violetta pulled out her bus pass. She stepped up on the wet metal slatted stairs into the bus, her heart lightening.

* * *

Geraldine woke up to a morning-warmed eider-down and a world outside her window that looked surprisingly sunny. She found her watch beneath a pile of books and scraps of paper on her bedside table – eight twenty-five. And the ferry that brought her to school on time left at seven-thirty. The next one she could catch now did not come until ten-past nine. Perhaps if her father were at home he would drive her down, so she wouldn't have to take the bus.

She stretched out her legs and shook her head a little. She felt better for the extra sleep, or was it just waking in the light and warmth instead of the cold darkness? Or the knowledge of the quiet, almost empty ferry trip ahead of her, instead of being full of uniforms and quarrels and minor confrontations?

She pulled herself out of bed, and wandered out towards the kitchen. Why had no one woken her up? Her father was sitting in the living-room on the green sofa, talking, or rather, booming away on the telephone. He looked very clean and

washed and was laughing while he talked. He beck-
oned to her to come over and sit next to him. He
squeezed her shoulders and laughed again, and
hung up.

'Well!' he said. 'Good morning! You're up late!'

'You didn't wake me!' Geraldine objected.

'I've got good news!' said her father, standing up
and pulling her with him. 'We've found a buyer
for the house!'

Was this good news?

'Oh,' she said.

Her father blew air from his puffed cheeks
theatrically, like cartoons of the West Wind. 'My
God, what a relief!' He rolled his eyes up to the
ceiling. 'I can't believe it.'

'When do we have to move?' asked Geraldine,
not feeling able to ask other questions, like who
was buying the house, and why was it such a relief,
and would they be very poor, and what was going
to happen?

But Geraldine's father did not seem to hear her.
He marched into the kitchen and poured himself
some coffee from its mottled silver percolator on
the stove, filling it with sugar and taking a grateful
swig.

'We should have a party,' he said. 'Why don't
we have a party?'

Geraldine shrugged. 'Will you drive me down to
the ferry?' she said. 'I've got to get the ten-past
nine.'

He heard that at least. 'With the greatest pleasure!' he declared.

Geraldine ate a wet tomato sandwich for breakfast, which she found in a paper bag by the sink – one of Violetta's rejects from the day before. Then she went out the back and pulled the guinea-pig cage over to a newish patch of grass for them to destroy. They screamed and disappeared at the sight of her, as usual. Ezra's guinea-pig manual had said that this was one of the most delightful attributes of guinea-pigs, how they always greeted their owner's approach with ear-piercing shrieks.

Ezra's house was silent and locked up – his parents would be at work, of course, and Ezra would have caught the seven-thirty. The little girl in the photograph was alone inside, waiting for them all to come home in the evening. Geraldine heard her father hooting the car on the road out the front, so she hurried in, picked up her bag, and ran out, bending over to tie up a shoe-lace and slamming the front door behind her.

No sign, she thought with a jolt, of the grey car and the two men inside it who had spent so long waiting for her parents last night. But just the memory of their visit made her shake with fear, like in old movies when the figure of death comes knocking at people's doors, with a black hood and cape and a big curving axe in his hand.

'Dad,' she said, as she strapped herself into the

front seat beside him, but that was as far as she got. He did not hear her, or at least, he did not answer her. He was whistling, and then he turned on the radio and opened the windows so the breeze spread out his long hair in a fine brown net.

She looked down at her feet, her scuffed black shoes with the shoe-laces in knots, and knew she would say nothing about it. If the two men wanted to see him, they would come back. Her father could deal with them. They were probably his friends, anyway. He often had friends to visit. Why should she find these two so sinister?

She tapped her father's arm to get his attention. 'Where's Mummy?'

'Gone into town!' he replied, with a strained smile. 'Up with the birds and off she went. What a priceless, marvellous mother you've got.'

He braked and turned into the deep street leading down to the water where a dozen or so shoppers and late starters were gathering at the wharf as the ferry rolled towards them in the distant dark-blue river.

'I know!' he said. 'Let's give her a birthday party! When did your poor mother last have a birthday party? Probably not since she was eight years old!'

Geraldine undid her seat-belt and leant over to kiss him goodbye. He smelt so clean and his blood was so warm, she felt a great, comforting love for him; his hands firm on the wheel, his mouth, though not his eyes, grinning. Despite all her own formless worries, she felt her heart lift and she smiled back. 'She'd love it!'

She got out of the car, pulling her school bag onto her back and breathed in the air rising from the water. She turned and waved as he did a circle and sped back up the hill.

13

Invitations

They were moving house. In a hurry.

There was so much to do: packing, sorting, discarding. Their mother never stopped. She slept in the same long fair plait that she wore during the day. She didn't seem to want any help. 'Leave it to me, girls,' she said. 'You've got your exams, Violetta, you mustn't get distracted.'

Geraldine had no exams, but she was grateful to be included in the sweep of this exemption. Removalists came from time to time, loaded up books, furniture, carpets, and took just about everything away. Violetta and Geraldine sat on the front verandah and watched strangers in green overalls carry off their belongings in the sunshine. Violetta brought them glasses of home-made

116

lemonade, which they co-operatively gulped down, and even asked for seconds.

Their things were being stored in a warehouse, their mother said. They might sell half of them, anyway. Depended where they ended up. Her sentences grew daily shorter and more pessimistic.

Their father was all over the place. Sometimes he packed and sorted and discarded too, but more often he was out, leaving scribbled messages of instruction here and there which no one ever found in time, mainly relating to what to say if a particular person called. But their mother was careful to get to the telephone first, and she knew what not to say. Then he would bang in through the front door and kiss whichever daughter happened to be in his way, hug her and say, 'How was school today?' then frown as he remembered something to tell their mother and bustle off again.

Geraldine did not look well. That's what she told herself when she looked into the stained mirror in their bathroom as she brushed her teeth. Her skin was yellow and her eyes red. Her lips were disappearing into her mouth, all the blood gone from them. Her teeth felt sore – should she tell someone? Every movement she made seemed to take so long. Even raising her toothbrush to her mouth had an agonising slowness to it. She could hardly bear watching the procession of the bristles through the air.

Alberta.

In the daytime, it was all right. Out in the sunlight Geraldine allowed herself to imagine that Alberta had come to a gruesome but deserved death in the suburban wilderness, her remains being digested by a local Doberman. Or, when she was in a kinder mood, that Alberta had passed on naturally in her sleep, her thick white body now rotting away in peace in a secluded niche of a neighbour's garden, to be dug up as a fossil by geologists in hundreds of millions of years and put in a museum and puzzled over and wondered at.

But at night, it was not so easy. At night, in Geraldine's dreams, Alberta became monstrous again. Her eyes grew unnaturally large, like a cat's, and her rodent teeth curled out of her mouth. Geraldine found herself staying up past midnight, afraid to fall asleep, listening to people talking on her transistor radio, and waking up exhausted the next day, the little red light of the radio still on and the faint morning mutterings oozing out of it.

If Alberta were still alive, though, where was she? How had she survived? Ezra's books said that guinea-pigs were vegetarians, so at least she hadn't been eating mice or destroying populations of endangered native cockroaches. Did she scurry over to Milly and Martha in their cage at night and mock them, like rabbits in *Watership Down*, urging them to escape and join her? Or was it possible she envied them, wished she could get back behind chicken-wire and have carrots and pellets brought to her, and snuggle up in a blanket with her fellow pigs? Geraldine knew what she would prefer, but Ezra said human responses were not a reliable guide to the feelings of animals.

She felt terrible about Milly and Martha. She had no idea what she was going to do with them. She had lied to her mother, told her that she'd found them a home, a girl at school who was very keen, and her mother had nodded and then obviously put them right out of her mind, crossed them off her list with a big black Texta.

Of course there was no girl at school. Geraldine had written a notice on the blackboard in yellow chalk on the section where they were allowed to write their own things (usually quotes of false wisdom found in desk diaries, such as 'Nothing is impossible', or 'Good things come to those who wait'). 'Two guinea-pigs need a home urgently. See Geraldine.' she wrote. It was a bloodless plea and no one responded. Perhaps she should have described them as 'sweet, fluffy, adorable', or added 'Get them before the butcher does.' (She'd read in Ezra's book how guinea-pigs are a delicacy in South America.) But somehow she wanted someone to take them regardless of their charms, just to take them because they were fellow creatures in need. But the twelve-year-olds in her class did not seem overly concerned with their fellow creatures in need.

Her father had not given up the idea of a party.

'Invite whoever you like,' he told them one evening as he stood in the kitchen cooking tomatoes and onions, and soggy pieces of fried bread. 'It'll be the last party we're having here, so you might as well go all the way.'

'Great!' said Geraldine co-operatively, hoping none of the mess in the pan was intended for her.

'For Mum's birthday?' asked Violetta, pouring herself a glass of ice-cold home-made lemonade, and glancing over at her mother who was reading sheets of grey paper. She smiled up at Violetta, but it was a tense, troubled smile. 'Just a party,' she said quickly. 'To say goodbye to the house. Do invite your friends.'

'Of course for Mum's birthday,' remonstrated their father, shaking a fork at their mother. 'And a house-cooling, as they call it, I suppose.'

'Where are we moving to?' asked Geraldine pointedly, because she knew Violetta would never ask.

'Ah, well . . .' Her father slipped the food from the frying-pan onto a large platter. He glanced over at their mother. 'We're not too sure yet. Might go and stay with your mother's cousin for a few weeks.'

Their mother's cousin, whose name was Deirdre, lived in a small house on the other side of the city.

'We won't fit!' said Geraldine. She shook her head as her father offered her some of the stew.

'She'll be overseas for a few months,' said their

mother, standing up. 'And your father might not be with us all the time, anyway.'

'Why not?' said Geraldine, ignoring Violetta's facial gestures ordering her to shut up.

'Might have to go away myself for a while,' said her father, trying to sound breezier than he looked. 'Poor old me, invalid that I am.'

'You shouldn't eat tomatoes,' mentioned Violetta. 'They're too acidic for your ulcer.'

'I cooked them for you, my Violet,' he protested. 'Build you up. Can't live off lemon juice. You've been looking far too much like your tragic namesake lately. Don't want you ending up like her.'

'For one thing, *that* Violetta was a prostitute,' Violetta said firmly, 'and for another, she died of tuberculosis. I can't see how she's like me at all.'

'Well, who's going to eat all this?' asked their father, theatrically glum. 'Smells so good, and none of you will touch it.'

'How about the guinea-pigs?' suggested Violetta unkindly.

'Ah, yes.' Their father was diverted for a moment. 'About those pigs, Gerry.'

Geraldine bit her bottom lip. 'What about them?'

'Well, what are we going to do about them? I don't know if Deirdre'll go for them.'

'I found them a home. I told Mum,' said Geraldine quickly.

'You could always take them back to the pet shop,' said Violetta, who did not believe in the existence of this 'home'. 'Like returning soiled goods.'

'They're not soiled,' retorted Geraldine. 'They look better than when I bought them.'

'Yes, but they must be a bit, well, used up, surely,' Violetta persisted, licking lemon juice from her lips. 'Their expiry date'll be coming round.'

'Funny, how Howard was so sure he saw that animal in the garden,' interrupted their father. 'You know, I thought I saw something myself a few weeks back. Remember, Violetta?'

'Oh yes, I remember,' said Violetta. 'Honestly, you'll be seeing unicorns next.'

Howard? Was that the name of the man with the beautiful shoes?

'Is that his first name or his second name?' asked Geraldine. 'Howard, I mean.'

Their father sat down, suddenly nervous, as if he had said something he wished he hadn't. 'Look, um, now that we're talking about it, you won't mention Howard's visit to anyone, will you? I mean, it's a delicate business, sales and so on. Okay?' He looked at them both anxiously. Geraldine shrugged. Who would she mention it to? Who would be interested, anyway?

'So he is buying the house,' she said, but her father did not answer.

'Not even the boyfriend, eh, Violetta?' was all he said, squeezing Violetta's shoulder. 'I'm sorry, what's his name again?'

'*Dad.*' Violetta was embarrassed.

Boyfriend. What a terrible expression.

* * *

Marcus came round after dinner, wearing furry green stockings that cyclists in Europe wear in the snow. Well, that's what he said when Geraldine couldn't help asking. He'd just taken his bicycle for a service at a bike shop round the corner from where they lived, so thought he'd drop in and invite Violetta to lunch for his mother's birthday.

'Oh! I can't!' Violetta was half regretful. Marcus's mother might go to a very delicious expensive restaurant for lunch, after all. Although perhaps not, remembering the orange-cream biscuits. They might just have a dull brown-bread sandwich at home. 'We're having a party here. For my mother's birthday.'

'Really?' said Marcus, turning his head to one side like a budgerigar.

'Well, yes,' confessed Violetta. 'Dad just mentioned it this morning. He said to invite you, by the way.'

'Ah.' Marcus looked gratified. 'Well, that will be nice. Things are improving, then, are they? Business-wise?'

Violetta looked at him sharply. How did Marcus know about the business? All she had told him was that they were moving house, nothing about the reason why.

'What about *your* mother's birthday?' objected Geraldine, who was sitting with them in the kitchen, drinking tea.

'Well, I could always take her for breakfast on the beach,' Marcus replied easily. 'She likes that sort of thing.'

Violetta looked at him, sceptical. 'Won't it be a bit cold for the beach? Windy?'

'Cold is a matter of taking precautions, darling,' said Marcus, patting his green legs.

'Why don't you ask her to come to our party?' Violetta said, unable to bear the thought of Marcus's poor mother huddled on the sand in green stockings eating gritty windswept birthday cake.

'Well, that's very kind,' replied Marcus, pleased. 'Your father won't mind an extra guest?'

'Oh no,' put in Geraldine, as she picked up a third chocolate-mint biscuit. 'He said to invite whoever we liked. As many as we liked.'

Violetta rolled her eyes at her sister.

'Ah.' Marcus paused, thoughtful. 'So Father can come as well, then? He'd enjoy it.'

Violetta stared. Did people's divorced parents go to parties together? Apparently they did. After all, she reasoned, they lived in the same house, didn't they? What was a party?

'Oh,' she said. 'Of course.'

Geraldine stood up. What a party this was going

to be. Deadly, by the sound of it. 'Got to feed the pigs,' she said, rather liking the effect of this laconic, farmer-like sentence. She'd always been fond of books about farms, where life was centred around feeding various animals, robbing them of their eggs and milk, then leading them to slaughter. Purposeful routine, not like getting up in the morning and going to school and coming home again. She stepped outside, pleasantly warmed by tea and chocolate. Who could she invite?

* * *

'Sad situation,' said Ezra's father, gesturing next door, as the video spun around.

'Hmmm. The less we know the better,' murmured his mother from her macramé. 'Can't go on much longer, anyway, from what they're saying.'

'What can't?' Ezra suddenly paid attention, something he rarely did to his parents' conversations. He was sitting on the floor, rolling his mother's ball of macramé wool about, as if he were a kitten.

His father coughed and rubbed his nose.

'That's what people do just before they're going to tell a lie,' mentioned Ezra. 'We learnt about it in school. It's body language.'

'I see,' said Ezra's father, shifting in his chair. 'What about pulling on the ears?'

'What can't go on much longer?' Ezra insisted.

'Geraldine's father's been having financial problems,' said his mother, calmly. 'It's not going well for him.'

'I wouldn't mention it to Geraldine, though, Ez,' put in his father. 'It might upset her. Don't know how much she knows.'

'I don't think she knows anything,' said his mother. 'Or Violetta, by the look of her. Head in the clouds, those two girls. I don't think they've been told anything.'

'Well, how do *you* know?' asked Ezra.

'It's been in the paper, actually.' Ezra's father coughed. 'But your mother's right. I wouldn't say anything. Their parents might not want them to know, you see, Ez. Might just worry them.'

'But now that it's in the paper,' sighed Ezra's mother, shaking her head. 'They'll have to find out, sooner or later.'

'Just a small paragraph at the back,' protested Ezra's father. 'I wouldn't have bothered reading it except that the name caught my eye.'

Ezra agreed with his father. Geraldine would never read a newspaper, apart from the comics, and if there were any spare room in Violetta's capacious brain, he could not see her filling it up with ephemeral things like the news.

The doorbell rang. They had one of those electric doorbells that go ding-dong, like cues on television comedies. Ezra's parents frowned at each other, although not with displeasure.

'Go and get it, will you Ezra?' said his father.

'I'll go,' said his mother. She laid down her cream-coloured lacework, and went to the door. Ezra scuttled to his room. He didn't particularly like visitors; not even the ones he invited himself.

'Ezra! It's Geraldine!' Ezra let his hand drop from the doorknob. So much for privacy. Slowly he came out to the living-room.

'Sit down, Geraldine,' his mother was saying. 'Near the heater. You look freezing. What have you been doing?'

Geraldine sat down on the sofa. Why had she come? She looked quickly over to the sideboard at Tory's photo, and felt herself relax slightly, as if she had just spotted someone she knew at a party. She said nothing, not even 'hello' to Ezra. She suddenly felt terribly tired, so tired she wasn't sure she could even open her mouth.

Ezra stared at her. Geraldine always looked strange, but tonight more than ever. Was it something to do with that guinea-pig, he wondered, or could it be she had found out something about her father and what his parents had just been talking about?

'Ezra, why don't you boil us all up a hot drink?' suggested his father, who also seemed disturbed by Geraldine's appearance. 'Some of that nice hot caramel milk of yours.'

'All right.' Ezra retreated obediently to the kitchen. At least he wouldn't have to talk to her.

As long as his parents didn't mind her sitting there like a lump of wood. But wood was not the right word – there was something unstable about Geraldine tonight. She was more like a pile of leaves on a still day, that as soon as the slightest breeze blew by would disappear into a thousand crackling irretrievable pieces.

'So, Geraldine,' said Ezra's father, wondering if he should turn the television off, or if perhaps a viewing of *Paint Your Wagon* might not do Geraldine the power of good. 'How have things been?'

Geraldine stared at the screen through the dim light, listening to Ezra's parents' gentle breathing, like a colony of sleeping bats. She sat herself down on a stool next to Mr Perlman, who seemed to exude some intangible masculine comfort, quite unlike her own father.

'Are you feeling all right?' asked Ezra's father.

Geraldine looked up at him, and found her sore eyes filling with tears at these words of unexpected kindness. But through some effort of nature she managed to send them back to their source.

'Would you like to come to a party?'

* * *

Marcus had left, striding busily off into the night to fetch his bicycle. Violetta's notes on *The Wife of Bath's Tale* lay neatly on the top of her desk. Violetta herself lay, not so neatly, sprawled across her unmade bed. She could fit in another hour's study before eating anything, although she admitted to herself that her mind was not at its most receptive. But Violetta did not believe in giving way to such excuses – that would be the beginning of the end, and she would wind up slobbing around in front of the television night after night like Geraldine.

So, she'd invited Marcus and his parents to the party, she thought with a groan. She hadn't meant to. Violetta had not wanted to invite any of her friends. She hadn't felt like talking about the fact they were moving house, and why they were moving, although sometimes she had the uncomfortable feeling that perhaps her friends, even her teachers, knew about it, from the way they looked at her, or the odd whispers or comments they made. Almost as if they knew even more than she did. Violetta ignored them.

Anyway, the least she could do was invite poor Marcus's mother. Violetta had a natural sympathy for mothers, rather the way some people have a natural sympathy for coal-miners or firemen, mindful of the awful working conditions and dangers of the profession. To be Marcus's mother, that would really be difficult.

She decided after all that it was dinner time. She went out into the kitchen, and found in the fridge half a takeaway pizza, still in its box. Whatever would they do without melted cheese, she wondered, darkly picking off all the pieces of pineapple (unfortunately Geraldine, when making the order, had forgotten how it made Violetta's mouth go all tingly). They would have starved. That sort of remark would irritate Marcus, making him cite endless examples of cultures who never touched dairy products and were healthier by far than any in the Western world. But, thought Violetta with a certain satisfaction as she bit into the icy pizza, Marcus is not here . . .

'Hello there!'

Violetta jumped and swallowed a large piece of crust in surprise. She turned around. At the door stood Simon.

'Um, the front door was open,' he said. 'I noticed as I was passing. On my way to visit Ezra, you know. Sorry.'

'That's all right,' said Violetta, gasping for air. 'Geraldine must have left it open. My sister. Geraldine.'

'Ah.' Simon stood at the door expectantly.

'Come in,' said Violetta. 'Unless Ezra's waiting for you.'

Simon stepped in eagerly. 'How are you?' he asked.

'Oh, all right,' replied Violetta. 'We're moving house, you know.'

'Yeah, I know. Ezra told me.' He was silent. Waiting. But Violetta waited too. After all, Simon was the one who dropped by. He must have something to say. But all he said was, 'Um . . .'

'Yeah,' she answered.

'Um,' he repeated.

'So we've been busy packing. You know.'

'Right.'

'We're having a party, actually,' broke in Violetta, without much effort, as Simon was not exactly monopolising the conversation. 'My mother's birthday. And a house-cooling, you know.'

'Ah.'

'Yeah.'

'When?'

Violetta, slightly taken aback, said, 'Sunday.'

'Oh.'

'Would you like to come?' Violetta found herself driven to say.

'Oh.'

The second 'Oh' was definitely more animated than the first.

He paused. 'Oh. Thank you. Yes. I'd love to come.' He paused again. 'The only thing is . . .'

'Yes?'

'Would it be all right if I brought my aunts? I promised to go with them to the aquarium on Sunday.'

'Oh.' It was Violetta's turn to stop and think. 'Well, perhaps you'd better do what you promised. They might be disappointed.'

'Oh no, not at all,' Simon assured her, rather too blithely, Violetta felt. 'I'm sure they'd far rather go to a party than look at a whole lot of ghastly fish. Well, I don't mean ghastly, exactly,' he added quickly. 'I mean, they're very interesting, especially from an evolutionary point of view.'

'Oh yes,' supplied Violetta, as Simon seemed to expect her to say something.

'I mean, you're interested in evolution, aren't you?'

Oh. Was she?

'When I saw you in the bookshop that time, with *The Origin of Species* . . .' Simon's voice trailed off into uncertainty. 'I mean, I was actually going to ask you to come with us, that's why I dropped in . . .'

Violetta took pity on him. 'Bring your aunts,' she said. 'If you think they'd like to come.'

'If you're sure that's all right . . .'

'Dad said to invite everyone we knew.'

What have I done? thought Violetta. Marcus and his parents. Simon and his aunts. How am I going to entertain them? Perhaps they could play Monopoly, or some very complicated card game that requires a lot of concentration. Marcus would be sure to know something like that, and be very good at it. While Simon, she was equally sure, would be quite hopeless.

'I'd better be going then,' suggested Simon.

'Well, yes,' agreed Violetta. 'I suppose Ezra will be wondering where you are.'

Still carrying her plate of cold pizza, she saw him out the door. If she had stayed to see him out the gate, she would have noticed, and been rather puzzled, that Simon did not proceed to Ezra's house, but headed straight up the road in the direction of the bus-stop.

But Violetta was too hungry to wait. She took her pizza into her bedroom and lay down in bed, wrapping herself up in her orange floral sheets like a baby in tight swaddling.

14

Discovery

The Sunday morning of the party, Ezra was up early. As he poured himself some muesli for breakfast (the toasted, very sweet kind that was like eating a bowl of crushed up Anzac biscuits with milk), he looked out over the garden next door in surprise. There were people out there; strangers, warmly dressed, marching about and setting up tables and chairs. Geraldine's party, of course.

Strange, to have a party when her father was going bankrupt, and worse by what he had read in a thin, grey column in the dull financial pages of the Saturday paper. He hardly understood what he read, but he recognised the name of Geraldine's father and that it was bad. It wasn't just that he had gone bankrupt, it was worse. He had broken the law. He was in league with criminals. He had stolen money. There would be a court case.

Ezra walked out the back door in his socks with his bowl of cereal and sat on a picnic bench on the porch and stared over the fence. Geraldine's backyard was big; twice as big as his, just as her house was twice as big. He supposed it would sell for a lot of money, and then her father would be rich again and pay back all the money he had stolen. Who had he stolen it from? It was not at all clear. It seemed to be from buildings rather than people. How do you steal money from a building? Could a building own money?

Money was something of a mystery to Ezra. It seemed to him that once you started getting rich, all it did was cause you trouble and get your name in the newspaper, like in ancient Greece, or was it Rome, when notorious citizens were ostracised, and had their names put up in public places and were sent away from the city for years and years and years. His own parents never talked much about money. Not that sort of money. They might mention that the price of milk had gone up, or how much did Ezra need for his textbooks. Perhaps, thought Ezra, you only found money interesting if you had a lot. Otherwise, really, it was rather dull . . .

'Hey! What's this?'

One of the women lugging the tables around was bending over Geraldine's guinea-pig cage, peering at the blue blanket.

'Rabbits?' said a man with a pile of chairs on his shoulders. He plonked them down on the dew-wet grass and came over to the cage. He pushed the wire slightly with his boot, to see if there was life inside, and one of the pigs – Milly? – poked out her moist trembling nose and squealed.

'Guinea-pigs,' he said. 'Give me a hand, and we can move them over to that corner.'

Just then, Geraldine emerged from the back door in her dressing-gown and moccasins, and scurried over to them. 'I'll move them!' she said, anxiously. 'Sorry!'

'That's all right,' replied the woman, looking at Geraldine kindly. She had huge dark pink cheeks and Ezra couldn't help thinking again how very yellow Geraldine was, as he held the cereal bowl to his lips and drained the last sweet drops of milk. The pink-cheeked woman helped Geraldine shift the cage over to the far back corner of the yard.

'Did we wake you?' asked the woman. 'You better go inside, you'll catch cold dressed like that out here.'

Geraldine said nothing, but pulled from her dressing-gown pocket some pieces of carrot and brown-edged, slimy lettuce, and put them inside the cage. From her other pocket she emptied a cascade of guinea-pig pellets. Geraldine shivered, the wet ground soaking her slippers. Her toes were so cold, it almost hurt to move them. She should go inside.

Ezra watched her, but she did not see him, not even look his way. Who would move in after they'd gone, he wondered. Was it possible that he would miss Geraldine? You got used to things, even things you didn't particularly like. Like a battered old car they'd had once; it was always breaking down and making his mother cry at traffic lights. Now when she saw the same model pass them on the street, she would sigh sentimentally and say to Ezra, 'Remember that terrible old car we had?' Perhaps in time he would come to feel this about strange, freckled, yellowing Geraldine.

'Um, Ezra?' He started and raised his head quickly from his father's cactus garden, which he had been staring at while he thought. It was Violetta, very warmly dressed, perhaps even over-dressed, in what appeared to be purple ski clothes. She was not wearing her glasses, but still managed to look preoccupied.

'Gerry told me she'd invited you to the party today.'

Ezra nodded. 'Well, my parents, but I suppose she meant me as well.'

'Are you coming?'

'I guess so,' he replied cautiously. Violetta seemed anxious, and other people's anxiety always made him suspicious.

'Oh, great!' Violetta beamed in relief. 'Because,

you see . . .' She sounded embarrassed. Ezra waited. 'Well, I invited Simon and his aunts, you see, and I was worried they wouldn't know anyone, you know, to talk to.'

'Simon and his aunts,' repeated Ezra in amazement.

'But if you and your parents are going to be there, well, that's all right then. You're all friends, after all.'

'Well, colleagues, really,' began Ezra, fearing rightly that the word 'friend' in this instance might have unfortunate consequences. But Violetta had disappeared down the side, leaving only the squeaking sound of her ski clothes rubbing against their various surfaces as a reply.

Should he tell his father about the aunts? Definitely not, Ezra decided. Then he might very well refuse to go to the party, leaving it to Ezra and his mother, while he enjoyed an afternoon dozing in front of *Paint Your Wagon*.

But Ezra had little idea of the forces of curiosity that drew adults to each other at times of scandal and crisis. Nothing, almost, could have made Ezra's father stay at home that afternoon, not even the prospect of Simon's relentlessly humane aunts.

• • •

Violetta, skipping out the front gate, did not notice the grey car that had been parked outside her house next to the caterer's van. Thank heavens for Ezra and his parents, she thought. She dashed up the street towards the shops on the next corner block.

She needed a pack of cards. Because she realised that all of their playing cards were packed away in that mysterious warehouse, and how would she ever get Marcus and Simon's aunts playing gin rummy without them?

The newsagent, she hoped, would have cards. That was the sort of useful emergency item you might expect to find in a newsagent, along with tubes of coloured glitter and tin boxes of fish-hooks. They would have a pack, tightly wadded in plastic, made in China with a coloured picture of a fox-hunt on the back.

But she never got in the front door to find out. Because outside the shop lay a pile of yesterday's papers, waiting to be collected or thrown away. The various lobes of the thick Saturday paper had become confused, and on the top of the pile sat the fierce financial section, without photographs, cartoons or even advertisements to lighten the weight of the type. As Violetta stepped up to go inside, her eyes fell down on the page, for no reason other than they had to look somewhere. But it was long enough for her to see it.

She saw her own surname, in the black letter of the narrow headline. If you see your own name, it's natural to take an interest, even if it can have nothing to do with you. So Violetta stopped.

And she read the words, her fingertips trembling.

··· 15 ···

The Party

The guests began arriving at about half-past twelve. Geraldine was in her room. She peered out her window at them, hiding. Her father was booming away as people arrived, welcoming, kissing, grabbing hands between two of his. Geraldine had noticed before how noisy her parents' friends were. They had deep, intrusive voices that reached into every crevice of the house. Even saying hello, they shouted.

People say children's parties are noisy, but in Geraldine's experience, children had nothing on her parents' friends. Children arriving at parties she had been to were usually too intimidated even to say happy birthday, but disappeared into the garden soundlessly as snakes. They yelled and screamed later on, of course, but at least when the food appeared they became silent again, like babies sucking at the breast. Whereas food and drink only seemed to pep adults up.

She wondered what her guinea-pigs would make of all this activity. Would they be scared, like dogs on fireworks night? And what about Alberta, if she was still alive, that is. Lurking in some deep, deep, dark burrow, where her pink eyes shone and she rolled herself up in a ball, chewing on a delicious vegetable salvaged from a garbage can, pausing to belch from time to time in general self-satisfaction. It really didn't bear thinking about.

Her mother was out the back with the caterers. Last time Geraldine looked, the long tables had been laid with blue and white tablecloths with hard papery corners, and food, plates and plates of food spread about on top. Vegetables, bowls of green and white dip and odd-shaped crackers, rolls of red meat with toothpicks through them, huge olives like plums, mussels on biscuits, caviar, little bits of scrambled egg on tiny pieces of toast, like something for a doll's tea-party.

And there was more food waiting in the kitchen. Hot dishes in great big pots, bread buttered and sprinkled with herbs. Not to mention the cakes. Flans with glazed fruit, cheesecakes with glazed fruit, and just plain glazed fruit. How many people were going to come? It seemed an incredible bounty, like something out of a fairy-tale.

Only once before had her parents had a party with a caterer like this. It was years ago, something to do with a business triumph of her father. She remembered how much food had been left over, how she and Violetta had crept out after everyone had gone and their parents were in bed, and attacked the scraps (well, you could hardly call such delicious, thick remains 'scraps') with their bare fingers.

There had been something magical about that food: enchanted, colourful and aromatic. Would it turn them into toads or statues? Would it make them dissatisfied with everything else they ate afterwards? Of course, none of these things happened. The next morning they simply felt sick from too full, too small stomachs. But Geraldine had not forgotten it, and the sight and smells of this feast reminded her again, and made her nauseous.

She heard Violetta leave her room and go down to the corridor to the toilet. Why wasn't she out the back with the guests? Violetta liked parties; she could always think of things to say to adults. She was so polite, she had the most well-mannered laugh and people inevitably liked her and thought her charming. That Violetta found being charming something of a perpetual strain never entered Geraldine's head, and this was a tribute to Violetta's gift, really. that she appeared to be enjoying herself when secretly she wasn't at all.

But Violetta, after washing her hands, went

straight back to her room, shutting the door quickly and firmly, turning the key in the lock. It was definitely odd. Had she even changed her clothes, wondered Geraldine? She would have to come out when Marcus and his parents arrived, not to mention Simon and his aunts.

Geraldine had not changed her clothes – at least, she had changed out of her pyjamas and soggy slippers into jeans, a jumper and desert-boots. But she hadn't put on any party clothes. She didn't have any, really, not since she had abandoned the party dresses of three or four years ago. No one would be missing her out the back, anyway, she had no charm at all. But Violetta . . .

'Violetta!'

It was their mother. She sounded strained. Geraldine heard footsteps treading down to Violetta's room, and her white hand knocking on Violetta's door.

'Violetta, Marcus is here.'

The key turned, the door opened, and a wordless Violetta emerged, closing the door behind her. Geraldine could sense through the plaster and brick of their walls their mother's puzzlement. She poked her head out to the corridor, but saw only the retreating back view of their mother's thick golden plait, bouncing off her shoulders like the beautifully groomed tail of a prize pony.

In the hall, Marcus was reintroducing his parents to Violetta, and three additional guests – Oliver,

Joseph and William – he'd brought with him, doubtless mindful of Geraldine's assurance that they'd been told to invite everyone they knew. Marcus was wearing traditional Nigerian dress, a long striped multicoloured shift reaching down to his feet. Well, further than his feet, as Marcus was not particularly tall, and this dress had presumably been designed for long, lean Nigerians.

'Happy birthday,' said Violetta to Marcus's mother. Marcus's mother produced from her handbag a small pink plant in a pot and said, 'And happy birthday to your mother, my dear. I've brought her a little gift.'

'Oh, thank you!' said Violetta, close to tears. 'I don't know where she's gone . . .'

'That's all right,' said Marcus's mother, patting Violetta's pale upper arm. 'Just put it aside and she'll find it later.'

They stood in the hallway for a moment, awaiting instructions from Violetta, as the hostess, to direct them to where 'it' was happening. But poor Violetta stood there blankly, as if she were waiting for them to tell her what to do, so at last Marcus, who could not be subdued for long, clapped his hands together and said, 'Well, let's move through, shall we?' And for once, Violetta was grateful for Marcus's so often grating mastery of things.

Geraldine had no wish to talk to Marcus, his friends or his parents. She was hungry though, and now Violetta was out there, her father was likely to be occupied introducing her to people, and he would leave Geraldine alone, perhaps not even notice her skulking about the laden dishes.

Geraldine avoided the hall, where guests continued to arrive, but squeezed through the laundry, out the side wire-screen, and jumped down the couple of concrete steps leading to the garden.

To her surprise, Ezra was already there, salvaging food slyly from the tables himself.

'How did you get here?' she asked, rather rudely, Ezra felt, as she had been the one to invite them.

'We came down the side,' he replied, spitting an olive stone into his hand. 'Do you mind if I drop this on the ground? It might grow into a tree one day.'

'Well, I won't be here to see it,' said Geraldine, sniffing, picking up a slice of rolled meat and putting it quickly into her mouth. Ezra was very well dressed, she noticed, with a clean white shirt and even a tie, and shiny brown shoes visible under his long khaki trousers. He looked like he was going to be awarded a prize by the Duke of Edinburgh.

Ezra knelt down and pushed the seed into a patch of dirt. There were many such patches on the grass, because of the guinea-pigs.

'Do you know who's moving in when you leave?' he asked, conversationally.

But Geraldine was as uninterested in talking to

him as he was to her, and she only shrugged. She wondered, though. Could it really be Howard who was buying the house? Like Violetta, she had her doubts about that man. Perhaps he was buying it for someone else to live in. She did not think they would see him at the party. When Geraldine closed her eyes, she saw rows of yellow and red question-marks, shuffling up and down in the black-ness. They made her head ache. So she made a point of keeping her eyes open, and picked up two more slices of meat. He'd better not say anything about being a vegetarian, she thought, chewing ferociously.

Geraldine's parents were standing together. Normally at parties they moved about from guest to guest, chatting, laughing, talking about food, but not today. Geraldine's father was holding tightly onto her mother's hand, like statues on married people's graves that only a chisel could break apart. In his other hand he held a glass of sparkling water, almost as tightly. His long hair fell into his eyes, but he wouldn't take his hand from her mother's to wipe it back.

At the opposite end of the garden, Ezra's father was staring at Marcus with a mystified expression on his face.

'Who's the guy in the dress?' he asked his wife, in a voice not quite as soft as it might be.

'Shhh,' she murmured. 'That's Violetta's boy-friend. Marcus. You know.'

'Ah,' said Ezra's father.

Geraldine, with a handful of chips, went and sat under the willow tree, leaning back against the trunk, watching. Marcus's friends had very rapidly and sensibly abandoned him, and were talking with guests of her parents, while Marcus had launched himself upon Ezra's mother, addressing her on some serious subject apparently to do with his outfit, for he was holding the edge of it for her inspection between his thumb and forefinger. Ezra's father had disappeared.

What was wrong with Violetta? wondered Geraldine. She was dressed up in her normal party way, but her face, her hands, her eyes were not Violetta, not the Violetta that presented on public occasions. She was hardly smiling, she was not nodding and agreeing. She seemed to strain even to hear whatever it was Marcus's father was saying, despite the fact he had such a loud voice it must have been clearly audible three houses down.

'Of course, in the late nineteenth century, the rapid development of the rudder was not in any way unforseen . . .' said Marcus's father, in the tone of a person making an obviously controversial pronouncement, for which he knows he will be immediately shouted down and derided.

Oh, why did I bring the subject up, thought Violetta desperately. Why didn't I stick to the weather, or the garden? And why does she just stand there saying nothing? How can she put up with it? There's no rule of etiquette, is there, that says you have to be just as patient with your husband after you divorce him as you did before? But then – and the thought burst through her distracted melancholy – perhaps she didn't want to get divorced, perhaps it was him. Perhaps she loves him terribly, and he broke her heart by moving upstairs. Violetta's own too-gentle heart heaved with flowing blood, and she felt overcome with a terrible generalised pity . . .

'Wasn't it?' she said, hopelessly.

'How do you do?' said Marcus's father. 'Pleased to meet you.'

Violetta frowned. What did he say? 'How do you do?'

She turned around. It was Simon's aunts. They did not speak in unison, nor did they hold out their hands at the same time, but somehow they gave the impression that they did. Violetta noticed Ezra's father lurking behind them, his neck bent as if held on a leash. They had caught him in the kitchen with a glass of punch.

'Lovely day for a party,' remarked one of the aunts, driven to such a blatant lie, no doubt, by Violetta's failure to perform the required introductions. For the sky had been greying over for several minutes now, the ground was damp, and people had goose-bumps on their exposed skin.

'Yes, well, it doesn't do to be too hot at these sorts of gatherings,' replied Marcus's father doubtfully. 'Heat-stroke, that sort of thing, you know.'

Violetta felt she would quite welcome a few dramatic cases of heat-stroke, someone fainting behind her so she could rush to the phone to call an ambulance.

'Where are your poor parents?' whispered one aunt with theatrical discretion to Violetta, who knew what she meant now, of course. But all Violetta said was, 'Is Simon here?' finding comfort in the soft, biblical syllables of the name. 'Simon?'

The aunts gestured in various directions, as if to say that Simon, like God, is always with us, which was probably true, seeing he was so dependent on them for a lift. Violetta looked wildly around her, but could see him nowhere. That's rather like God, too, she thought dolefully, recalling the phrase from the Bible: 'Seek and ye shall find', which had always struck her as a most profound untruth. But without a word she obeyed its instructions, and wandered away into the crowd of people, searching.

Ezra walked slowly and carefully over to where Geraldine was sitting, holding a half-full wine glass of Coca-Cola in his hand, and carrying a plateful of potato and dill salad. He sat down next to her, and pulled a knife and fork wrapped in a serviette from his top pocket. He settled himself against the tree trunk and began to fork the vegetables into his mouth.

He sneaked a glance at Geraldine. If before she looked yellow, now she almost looked blue. Her eyes were staring straight ahead of her, and crumbs of barbecue potato-chip were spread about her mouth, which she licked off slowly with her greyish tongue. Whoever compared a person's tongue with a ripe strawberry had never seen Geraldine's.

Inside, a radio was turned on. Some rather mournful choral music burst through the low window of the dining-room. It softened and loudened and softened again, giving the impression of shaking foundations, it sounded so deep and important. Then it stopped and there was the whizzing noise of someone changing channels rapidly, through discussions of sport, news, pop music, orchestras. Finally it stopped at a song, something operatic.

Geraldine closed her eyes, as the deep crackling old-fashioned voice of someone who must have died years ago cried its eternal sorrows about their devastated garden. Some people find consolation in music, she knew, like her father and his guitar. The trunk of the tree dug into her back, cold and wet, but she found its presence, even the pain it caused, reassuring. She felt almost peaceful.

Just as the song was finishing, there was a loud knocking at the front door. The radio was abruptly turned off. Another late guest, Geraldine thought sleepily, come for the leftovers. She was aware of her parents, of people, walking away, of a hub of low talking. But she didn't move, she stayed dozing, stomach pleasantly full. It wasn't warm, but the rain had staved off. She felt her head sink slowly forward, echoing strains of music rising above her . . .

··· 16 ···

The Strangers Return

'Geraldine! Geraldine!'

She opened one eye. Ezra was shaking her shoulder.

'What?'

'Everyone's gone inside,' he said.

'So what?' she retorted, and yawned. There was a hush, and an emptiness in the garden. The caterers stood by the tables of food, murmuring. One of them shovelled egg and mayonnaise onto a plate. The woman with the bright red cheeks was looking at Geraldine, concerned.

'I think you better go indoors, pet,' she called. 'Go and see your dad.'

Geraldine frowned. 'What happened? Where is everyone?'

153

'Inside,' said the red-cheeked woman, who was perhaps a little less ruddy than she had been.

Geraldine turned to Ezra.

'Maybe your dad's making a goodbye speech or something,' he muttered.

Geraldine picked herself up from the ground. That brief feeling of fullness and contentment had disappeared. She noticed that her back was cold and aching slightly, that she was starting to get a sore throat. She blinked and sniffed and said to Ezra, 'Oh well, let's go in then.'

They walked in through the laundry, now empty of baskets and machines, and into the kitchen. There was no sound of a speech. People were standing about, talking softly. When they saw Geraldine, they touched her on the shoulder, they pushed her through the doorway. Ezra's father stood by the stove, not talking to anyone, but when he saw Ezra, he grabbed hold of him, and held tightly onto his hand.

Geraldine passed slowly into the deep, high hallway. What was going on? People stood about here as well, and she could hear her mother crying somewhere – in the bedroom? The living-room? Where was her father? Where was Violetta? She swung around, then stopped still, in shock.

The two men. The two men in the dark-grey suits. The two men she had opened the door to and sent away that night. They stood at the stairwell. They did not look at her, they looked at the ground. They were waiting.

Her father came out from behind the dining-room doors, her mother behind him. Surely Geraldine had heard her crying, but her eyes were dry and dark. Her father approached the two men.

'I don't want her to come with me,' he said, gesturing at Geraldine's mother, and they nodded.

'Right, sir,' said one of them.

Geraldine's father caught sight of her. He leant towards her and kissed her hair. 'I'll be back in a couple of hours, my love,' he said. 'Where's Violetta?' He looked sad, but not surprised.

Geraldine shook her head. What's happened, she wanted to say, where are you going? Who are they? But she said nothing.

Her father turned to her mother. He did not kiss her, but he touched her thick golden plait with the tips of his fingers, as if it were Rapunzel's braid, and had some magical restoring power that might save him, whisk him away to a tall tower with her, away from the men in grey suits and the staring greedy eyes of his friends. Then he walked with the two men, one on either side, out the front door.

No one spoke for a moment, like that short, unstable silence in church the moment after the minister glides out the back door. Then someone whispers, someone else replies, people start to move about, collect their belongings, talk more loudly, even laugh.

Geraldine, who had watched the exit of her

father in a frozen trance, suddenly came to life and dashed out the door after him. She ran to the gate and onto the footpath, where he was getting into the back of the shiny car. Other people followed her, from inside the house. Ezra was there, she knew that much. She did not see him, but she was aware of his shape, his colour, his presence near her.

The grey car was parked in front of their driveway. Geraldine could not bear it. They must tell her what had happened. What was going on? She felt herself panicking. Her father turned and smiled at her, and mouthed some words as obscure to her as a foreign language. She shook her head. Her lips were sore where she had been licking salt from them in the cool wind.

'What's happening?' she shouted, stamping her feet.

There was a small crowd of people gathered in front of the house. Not just party guests, but also people from other houses, who had been digging in their front gardens or reading the newspaper on the verandah and had come over to see Geraldine's father as he was driven away. But none of them said anything.

'Geraldine! Look!'

Someone pulled her by the arm, insistently. It was Ezra, his eyes shining. Like Tory's, she thought, automatically. She looked to where he was pointing.

'Look!' he breathed, like a visionary saint seeing Mary beaming at him in a dark grotto. 'It's her!'

Geraldine looked. She looked hard, with astonishment. She looked directly into two pale pink penetrating eyes. She looked at the long glossy fur, and the firm, unafraid whiskers, the bold, pale-brown nostrils. She looked into the eyes and Alberta looked out.

She was scarcely a metre away from where Geraldine and Ezra were standing. She was perched on a small lump of clay on the nature strip in front of their house. She was totally fearless; she was superior. She stared at the crowd, challenging. Geraldine was transfixed, immobilised by the steady, proud gaze. She heard the smooth grey car start its engine, warming up to take her father away, but she couldn't turn her head from Alberta. The car started to reverse.

'Alberta!' shouted Geraldine, jumping towards her.

Suddenly, shocked, Alberta lunged forward, as if someone had pushed her violently from behind. She shot out onto the driveway, towards the spinning black rubber of the tyres. Geraldine screamed, high, long and loud. Alberta seemed to bounce upwards, fell over on her back, straight under the wheels of the reversing car. Geraldine screamed again.

The car stopped and one of the men, the one driving, got out.

'Jesus Christ,' he said, and peered under the curving bumper bar.

Geraldine covered her eyes with her fingers. She felt her mother's arms about her and she hid herself in her mother's body.

The driver put his hand to the tyre and pulled at the white fur.

'Where did it come from?' he said, shaking his head. 'God, I'm sorry. Was it hers?' and he gestured at Geraldine.

Ezra stepped hesitantly forward and went over to the car. He knelt down next to the tyre and next to Alberta.

She was broken somewhere, her body was out of shape, but there was no blood on her fur. She was breathing very very fast, as if she had just finished a long race. This is how the runner must have looked who dashed all those miles from Marathon to Athens, thought Ezra, just managing to get out a message of victory before dying in the arms of his fellow-citizens.

Did Alberta have a message? Her poor pink eyes were half-open, and Ezra sensed an urgency about her. Perhaps it was only death. Because Ezra knew she was dying. So this is how it feels, he thought, when someone is dying, lying on a street, panting their final breaths.

The driver knelt down next to him.

'Should we get a vet or something, son?' he asked, but Ezra shook his head.

'She's dying,' he said.

'I'm so sorry,' said the man. 'I'm so sorry. Is it yours?'

'It wasn't your fault,' said Ezra. 'She just ran out. You couldn't know.'

The man leant over her. 'The poor little thing,' he said gently. 'Poor little thing.'

Ezra had forgotten the other people standing around. He was aware only of himself and Alberta. He raised his hand, and stretched it towards Alberta's coat, and, in a tentative gesture of unexpected and unpractised affection, stroked the yellowed, thorn-matted fur. Funny how in the twilight the first time he had seen her, she had looked so very white. Now under the cold afternoon sun, her fur was clearly stained with urine and grass, tangled like a wild, long-haired sheep. Her little face jerked to one side, her whiskers shook, her half-dead eyes glanced up at him, not unfavourably, he felt.

He watched as Alberta drew her last, rapid breath. Her life did not wind down slowly, as you might expect, but finished suddenly, between respirations. She just stopped breathing. The jerking movement at her chest ceased. Alberta was dead.

Ezra leant over and picked her up. He lifted her from the ground, and took her cooling body in his arms. He looked over at Geraldine.

But Geraldine, her head beneath her mother's

arm, kept her eyes tightly closed. She didn't want to see anything, hear anything, know anything. If only you could close your ears, she thought, like platypuses do when they go underwater. If only you could close everything off and just drift about in the silent, odourless dark.

17

True Love

So Geraldine's father was arrested, taken away by the two detectives, charged with fraud. And Alberta was found, run over, dead. The guests vanished, the party dissolved, the house and the family in ruins.

Violetta and Simon were in Violetta's bedroom. Violetta was lying on the bed, crying. Simon was less comfortably positioned on a splintery wooden box. They had been there for some time. It was getting dark. Violetta would not come out of her room.

At first Simon had tried arguing with her. 'Say goodbye to your father at least,' he'd suggested, but she'd turned on him with unexpected fury, that almost made him wish he were somewhere else altogether. But not quite.

'Never!' she said. 'I'm never going to talk to him again!'

'Oh,' said Simon.

'Never!' Violetta rolled over on her back. 'You know what he's done, don't you? Of course you know. Everybody knows. It was in the paper, wasn't it? Everybody knows except me.'

'Well, it was in the paper,' agreed Simon. 'But it was very small writing.'

'He's a thief,' muttered Violetta to her pillow. 'A thief, a thief, a thief, a thief.'

'Perhaps there were mitigating circumstances,' broke in Simon, fearing she might go on saying the word all night. 'You know, I mean, businesses and all that . . .'

Simon faltered, not actually knowing the least thing about businesses or the crimes you might find yourself committing if you got in deep enough. Were there mitigating circumstances, after all? He had not understood the newspaper report he'd read at breakfast in his college dining-room the day before, all the more interesting parts of the paper having been taken by the earlier risers. Bits he understood – the legislation breached, the large sums of money, the names of the other people involved. He had seen Violetta's father's name, and that he was likely to be charged with some kind of fraud to do with his toy empire and to do with other businesses. Howard someone-or-other seemed to figure largely, but it didn't appear that they had enough evidence to charge him.

Simon had been hoping, in fact, for Violetta to enlighten him about it all, she was so clever. He had imagined her declaring her father's innocence of all charges, assuring him that he was the victim of a cruel and elaborate conspiracy, and how she, his loving daughter, would stand by him forever no matter what anyone said or did, even if he went to prison for fifty years.

'I hate him! I hate him! I never want to see him again!' sobbed the loving daughter. 'I wish he was dead!'

Simon shifted on the splintery box. It was really very uncomfortable. He would have liked to go and sit next to Violetta on her bed, but he was afraid she might hit him.

'He's a liar! He's a thief!' wept Violetta and she continued in this vein for some time.

Simon, while not exactly growing weary of her company, which was a blessing under any circumstances, did start to wonder how he was going to get home, seeing his aunts had deserted him. Sunday was not a good day for public transport – but could he afford another taxi? He could hardly ask Violetta's mother for a lift . . . Could he?

'Where's my mother?' Violetta interrupted his thoughts telepathically, sitting up suddenly in bed, pushing back her tear-sodden hair. 'She didn't go with him, did she?'

'She knocked on the door a little while ago,'

mentioned Simon, 'but you told her to go away and that you hated her and you never wanted to see her again.'

'Did I?' Violetta looked unrepentant.

'Your father should be back soon, anyway,' said Simon, not sure if this would comfort her or not. 'They can't put him in prison without a trial, you know. Only charge him. Someone will have to pay bail, of course,' and he frowned. How do you pay bail if you're bankrupt? Simon had rather old-fashioned ideas of bankruptcy, drawn largely from the works of Dickens.

'Maybe they won't let him out,' suggested Violetta, brightening. 'They refuse bail sometimes, don't they?'

'Only if they think you're dangerous or you're going to run away.' replied Simon, firmly. 'I'm sure they'll let him out.'

Violetta fell down again on the bed.

'What happened to Marcus?' she asked.

'He knocked too,' said Simon. 'But you just sort of moaned, so he went away.'

And a good thing too, Simon told himself. Marcus was hardly the sort of person you wanted around in an hour of need, especially in that ridiculous dress, like Joseph and his Amazing Technicolour Dream Coat. How could Violetta be going around with him, as Ezra had claimed she was? It was an unprofitable line of thought, likely only to depress him.

164

He was beginning to feel rather hungry. He hadn't managed to eat much before the detectives had arrived and Violetta had gone into this spasm of outrage. She seemed such a calm sort of girl, too. Sharp, but calm. She'd been a little odd before the detectives came, admittedly, a bit distant and cranky, but the sight of the two suited men appearing at the wide open door and asking for her father had drained her of all normalcy. He wasn't sure now how he had been brave enough to follow this white-faced girl down the corridor to her room, nor, as she stumbled inside, why she had let him come with her, locking the door behind them and flinging the key on the floor.

'Why didn't she tell me?' she muttered to her pillow, sitting up on the edge of the bed. 'She should have told me.'

Because her mother had known, she was sure of it. It made sense of all those late nights and cryptic murmurs, that horrible Howard and his clean shoes. Violetta now knew she would never trust a man with clean shoes ever again in her whole life, and she took a quick look down at Simon's to reassure herself – yes, grubby runners with frayed laces. Very satisfactory.

'I suppose she didn't want to upset you,' said Simon. Or knew you'd dob him in, he thought, because Violetta turned out to have an unexpectedly vicious sense of justice.

Violetta went over to the door and tried the

handle, apparently forgetting she had locked it herself.

'Where's the key?' she snapped.

'Well,' began Simon.

That's when they realised the key was missing. Violetta had tossed it, or rather hurled it aside with such venom, that it seemed to have disappeared altogether. It was hard to understand how this was possible, as there was scarcely a plank of furniture left in the room, and no nooks or cracks where it could have fallen. But neither of them could see it anywhere. Simon thought back to when she had flung it away, and he was pretty certain it was in the right direction, but then he thought again and said maybe the left direction.

All the while Violetta became more infuriated, with him, chiefly, which he felt was unfair. He had been brought up never to lock your bedroom door. What if your pyjamas caught fire while you were asleep, or you knocked yourself unconscious against the wall as you turned a page reading in bed?

Violetta banged on the door a few times, and called out to Geraldine and her mother, but there was no answer. What could they do, anyway, ventured Simon, short of ringing a locksmith or breaking down the door with an axe.

'We'll just have to climb out the window,' said Violetta, with a withering glance. 'We can't stay here all night.'

'I suppose not,' agreed Simon reluctantly. 'And

it's not such a far drop, is it?'

He pushed open the glass into the branches of the camellia trees that grew under Violetta's window. The blooms had reached their least attractive stage where they turn brown at the edges and fall to pieces at the slightest touch. The drop to the dark earth below was only a metre or so. Simon lifted a leg over the window-sill like striding a horse, then let himself off, plop, into the softness beneath his feet.

As he did so, there was the sound of a car slowing down, a door opening and slamming shut, someone getting out.

The front gate clicked behind him. Simon turned and reached up his arms to help Violetta.

'Daddy!' Violetta shouted and leapt from the window straight past him, falling on her knees into the earth. She picked herself up and ran straight towards her father, who had just walked in the front gate. In the twilight, he had lost all colour. He looked grey – grey hair, grey clothes, grey skin.

'Violetta,' her father said softly, reaching out to her, and his voice was grey too. He hugged her to his shoulder.

Well, someone found the bail, thought Simon, lowering his arms and putting his hands into his pockets.

And he watched them, Violetta and her father, through the dying camellias in the dying light, walk together arm in arm into the house. The door banged shut in the wind behind them.

True love, thought Simon. He sighed, but he was not unhopeful.

18

Eyes Open

Geraldine lay on her back in bed. Her eyes had been shut from the moment she found her room after her father had gone away in the grey car. She had lain down, fully clothed, and closed her eyes.

She had heard Violetta, talking, crying, shouting, she had heard doors banging, voices of people she did not know, or had forgotten. Through everything she had kept her eyes shut, and finally there had been no noise at all, just the sounds of the garden, the wind, the leaves, the moving distance.

She lay in the darkness, very still. This is how a dead body must feel, she thought. She didn't think about her parents, or Alberta, or the two men. She felt the inside of her mouth with her tongue; her teeth, her palate, her gums. She lay listening to her blood flow, like a hibernating bear.

Her mother came in and took off her shoes, then pulled a blanket over her. She shook her shoulder a little.

'Darling,' she said.

Geraldine kept her eyes closed.

'Geraldine,' said her mother. 'Darling. Your father and I are going out. We have to go and talk to someone. We won't be long. I'm telling you so you won't be frightened. Everything will be okay.'

I won't be frightened, thought Geraldine. I'm not moving. I'm staying here.

'Violetta's gone out too,' said her mother. 'With her friend Simon.'

Yes, thought Geraldine. That's good.

'She said she wanted to go,' her mother said, sounding forlorn. She kissed Geraldine on the cheek. 'I'll see you soon.'

In the end, of course, Geraldine did get up. Perhaps an hour later. No one was home. Even the caterers had gone, taking every scrap of the party with them, every surface left clean and crumbless.

She went into the living-room, although you could hardly call it a living-room without any furniture, except for the small black-and-white television they were going to take to her aunt Deirdre's place. She lay on the floor on her stomach, smelling the dirt deep in the carpet beneath her.

There was a knock on the glass doors behind her. Her head jerked up, shot through with fear. But it was only Ezra. He stood there, in the dark part of the day, a package of some kind under his arms. Geraldine did not get up to let him in, so he twisted the door open himself.

'Geraldine?' he said, or rather, asked.

'What?'

Ezra paused. He looked sad. He did not often look sad. Small, thoughtful, disappointed, but not sad. 'I'm going to bury Alberta,' he said. 'Will you come with me?'

Geraldine sat up. 'Where?'

'Well,' said Ezra tentatively, 'I thought in our garden. I mean, we could bury her in yours, but you're leaving. I mean, if she's in mine, at least you know someone knows she's there . . .'

He stopped. Geraldine said nothing.

'Do you want to?' he asked. 'Geraldine?'

She got up from the floor and walked over to him. She pointed at the blue plastic parcel under his arm. 'Is that her?'

Ezra nodded.

She looked at him, suspicious. 'All right,' she said.

She stalked ahead of him, out the front door. The evening air was mild, the light dark-blue. She walked in her socks, straight past Ezra's house, down the side path into the back garden, Ezra and his package trailing behind her.

'Where abouts?' said Geraldine, when they reached the yard. She looked about, feeling the wet from the earth soak up to her toes. The cactuses in the dim light looked almost like alien creatures, animals themselves, huddled together in conspiracy. The greens were grey and they cast weak shadows over the stony earth.

Ezra pointed. Near the fence was a shallow ditch, recently dug, and a red trowel standing up in the earth beside it. Geraldine walked over and knelt down next to it. The ditch was not very deep as Ezra had never seen anyone buried, so he had no idea how deep a grave should be. For him, burying a body was like planting a seed.

He sat down next to her, holding the blue plastic parcel gently in both hands. Geraldine stared at it.

'What about a coffin?' she said.

'In Israel they don't have coffins,' said Ezra. 'They wrap you up in a flag.'

'Oh.'

'My cousin was buried there,' said Ezra. 'I saw pictures they sent us. He was a soldier.'

'Oh.'

There were a number of answers to this. Alberta wasn't a soldier, she wasn't even a person, this wasn't Israel. But instead Geraldine found herself saying, 'What about Tory? Did she have a coffin?'

Ezra was silent, except for a very deep lonely breath. Then he said, 'I don't know. I didn't see.'

'Didn't you go to her funeral?'

Ezra shook his head. 'No,' he said. 'I didn't even see her when she was dead. I didn't want to see her.'

'Why not?'

Ezra frowned, almost as if he had not asked himself this before now. He looked into Geraldine's face – was the answer there?

'I don't know,' he said slowly. 'I think I was afraid. I think.' He paused, then picked up the trowel. 'Well,' he said, 'let's do it.'

'I want to see her,' said Geraldine. 'I want to see her before we put her in.'

Ezra fingered the plastic gently. 'Open it up,' said Geraldine, and she repeated, 'I want to see her.' But she would not pull apart the plastic cover herself. Ezra's hands were trembling.

'All right,' he said. He folded the blue flaps to one side and the other, and uncovered Alberta. Poor, white, huge, dead Alberta. Still, very cold, stiffening, eyes open, whiskers flat. Dead Alberta. Shining Alberta. Remote, unknowable. Unmournable.

Geraldine stared. And stared. So this was Alberta. Last time she had been so close, she had been alive, scuffling inside a shoe box, eating a sandwich. And now . . . In her dreams, Alberta was monstrous. Violent and cruel. Out to get her. Now she was dead and so near, she was different. Vulnerable, small, short-sighted, tenacious, admirable. Geraldine stared. Warm-blooded, like herself. An animal, not a ghost.

'Oh!' Geraldine tightened her toes in her socks. She heard in her head the tyre sinking into Alberta's back.

Ezra stretched out his hand and laid it on Alberta's cold neck. He lowered his head, and rested his cheek against her fur. A surreptitious kiss crept out of his mouth. Geraldine didn't see. He sat up straight again, and wrapped her up.

'You put the earth,' he told Geraldine.

Geraldine took the trowel and pushed the dirt on top of the package, flattening it out and making it straight and neat, like a low sand-castle. She picked up some pebbles from around the cactuses and decorated the little mound with them. Ezra stood watching. When she had finished he helped her up from the ground, putting his clean hand into her muddy one.

'Are you still leaving on Wednesday?' he asked.

Geraldine shrugged. 'I suppose so. The house is sold. We have to leave. I mean, it doesn't make any difference about Dad being arrested.' You're under arrest. How ridiculous it was, thought Geraldine. A phrase from a cartoon, like 'Take me to Cuba!' or 'Hands up in the name of the law!'

There was a pause.

'What are you going to tell your friend about . . . Alberta?' Ezra spoke the name with difficulty.

'I just don't know. I really don't,' moaned Geraldine. She added, 'I mean, it was my fault.'

'Well, it was, really,' agreed Ezra, unhelpfully.

Geraldine scowled at him. 'Perhaps I'll send her round to see you,' she said. 'To visit the grave. You two'll probably get on like a house on fire.'

A glow suddenly grew over the garden, from out of Ezra's house, his father settling in for the evening's session of *Paint Your Wagon*. They could hear the faint music of the opening credits. Geraldine looked at Ezra; Ezra looked at the ground.

'Um.' Ezra chewed on his lips, thickly chapped from windy ferry trips. 'Would you . . .' He stopped. 'Have you . . .'

'What?'

'I mean,' said Ezra in a rush, 'if you haven't found a home for them, I could look after your guinea-pigs.'

Geraldine was shocked, and surprised to find she was still capable of it.

'But you're against pets!' she said. 'You hate caged animals.'

'I know, I am,' replied Ezra. 'I am. I do. But . . .'

Geraldine waited.

'Well, I mean . . . if you can't find anyone else . . .' he broke off lamely. 'I'll look after them, till you get a house where you can have them back.'

Would I ever want them back, wondered Geraldine. Such a marvellous escape Ezra was offering her. And he would look after them so well, she knew. He would be so responsible, much better than her. He would feed them and keep them clean, and keep an eye out for all sorts of rodent diseases and give them the very latest treatment. He might not offer them much spiritual comfort, of course, but they didn't want that. He would give them what they really wanted, without trying to get anything from them. Not like her. They would never disappoint him, because he would expect nothing.

Quite suddenly, she smiled at him, and he smiled back, perhaps the first genuine smile they had ever shared. 'Thank you, Ezra,' she said. 'It'd be wonderful.'

Wonderful. She repeated the word inside her head, for she felt she needed a word like that to help her through the future hours, days, weeks – would it be years? Would her father go to prison? Where were they going to live? A few months at her aunt Deirdre's and then what? Another house, perhaps another city, another school, another life . . . But at least now she understood more of what was happening, even if not when, or why, or how. And just knowing the little she did know made everything seem different, less formless, less frightening. She could open her eyes, and be less afraid of what she might see.

'I don't think I want to have any more pets,' she said at last.

'Oh yeah.' Ezra raised his eyebrows.

'You don't have to believe me,' snapped Geraldine. 'I don't care if you do or not.'

Her head ached with unshed tears. Her feet were cold, and her hands and elbows covered with mud. Wonderful? Not quite. But she resolved to shut away thoughts of the future for the moment. Just now, she needed to take her life slowly, understanding perhaps only one grain at a time. And she too, despite everything, was not unhopeful.

About the Author

Ursula Dubosarsky is widely regarded as one of the most talented and original writers in Australia today. She is the author of several outstanding books for children and young adults. Ursula has won many awards for excellence, including the 1994 Victorian Premier's Literary Award and the 1994 New South Wales State Library Award for *The White Guinea-Pig*. *The First Book of Samuel* won the New South Wales Premier's Ethnic Affairs Commission Award and was named an Honour Book in the 1996 Australian Children's Book of the Year Awards.

Ursula lives in Sydney with her husband Avi, her daughter Maisie, and sons Dover and Bruno.

MORE GREAT READING FROM PUFFIN

☆☆☆☆☆☆☆☆☆☆☆☆☆☆☆☆☆☆☆☆☆☆☆☆☆☆☆☆☆

ALSO BY URSULA DUBOSARSKY

High Hopes

Julia organises English lessons for her father at home, but little does she realise that her life is about to be turned upside down. Quietly, surreptitiously, Julia plots her revenge.

A Children's Book Council of Australia Notable Book, 1991.

The Last Week in December

Bella has a terrible, guilty secret, something she did three years ago when her English relatives were visiting. Now they are returning to Australia and Bella fears the worst . . .

The First Book of Samuel

On his twelfth birthday, Samuel Cass disappeared . . . A subtle and resonant story of identity and growth, by a truly original author.

Bruno and the Crumhorn   Ursula Dubosarsky

When Bruno is forced to learn a cumbersome, medieval musical instrument, little does he know the unlikely chain of events that will follow! Another highly original story from this talented author.

Zizzy Zing   Ursula Dubosarsky

When Phyllis spends the summer at an old convent school in the Blue Mountains, a mysterious letter arrives for her mother. Her desire to find the sender leads to a bewildering tragedy. Who is the strange lady she meets on the train, and what is the dark secret that torments her?

MORE GREAT READING FROM PUFFIN
☆☆☆☆☆☆☆☆☆☆☆☆☆☆☆☆☆☆☆☆☆☆☆☆☆☆☆☆

Bumface Morris Gleitzman

The hilarious and moving story of a blended family that seems to be growing out of control. When things start to get desperate, it's down to Angus to hold it all together.

Unseen Paul Jennings

Stare, if you dare, into Paul Jennings's wild world. Can the dead come back to life? Could you escape a man-eating ghost? Who are you if you are not yourself? Can you cheat the fate that awaits you? Eight new stories that you would never dream of. Masterful storytelling from the one and only Paul Jennings.

The Silver Fox Rosemary Hayes

After the death of her mother, Emily sees the silver fox, a vision that is said to warn people of impending danger. Emily becomes caught up in a race to prevent a tragedy she knows is about to happen . . .

The Listmaker Robin Klein

Sarah Radcliffe could easily be a contender for the least-popular-girl-in-the-school award. But all that's about to change when the glamorous Piriel Starr becomes her stepmother.

Shortlisted for the 1998 CBC Book of the Year Award for Younger Readers. Winner of the 1998 SA Festival Award for Literature (Children's Books).